Opal Field

Her

Scorched

Bones

Chapter 1

Jenny steered another drunken reveller away as he collided with her on the dance floor. More beer sloshed onto her foot, still throbbing from the cowboy boot stomping on it a few moments before.

Her whole body vibrated. Party goers bumped and swayed. Music blasted from a wall of speakers either side of the stage.

'I can't believe you talked me into this.' She leant close to Nev's ear so he could hear her.

Strobe lighting flashed across his face – his white teeth glowed iridescent against his dark skin.

'You need to learn to let your hair down a little Constable Williams.' A wave of hot flesh swam around them. She swayed to the music, as best she could, feeling awkward and uncoordinated. Her tall, gangly body was ungainly on a dance floor.

'There's letting your hair down and then there's going nuts. This is insane.' Jenny waved her hand around the scene. The smell of beer and sweat filled the air. 'I didn't think there were this many people living in the region, let alone so many singles.'

'A BnS ball brings them out of the woodwork, that's for sure.' He glanced up. 'Speaking of which.' He nodded behind Jenny. She checked over her shoulder.

Nick waved and the sheepish grin on his face made her realise this place was no more his cup of tea than it was hers. She wondered what brought him along. They were technically singles, or Bachelors and Spinsters as the B and S mantra required, but bars and clubs were the last place she expected to see the quiet, sombre cattle farmer.

Seeing Nick always made her think of her missing family. He was one of the few people who knew she came to Coober Pedy to find answers and now she believed his family could be the key to finding out what happened to Melanie and Aunt Carolyn, nearly a decade ago.

'Hi,' Nick shouted over the music.

'Hi yourself. I didn't expect to see you here.' Apart from being a hermit on his remote property, Nick only recently recovered from a gunshot wound – one she still felt totally responsible for.

'I heard you were coming.' He nodded toward Nev. There was no point glaring at her roommate, he was already distracted chatting up a blonde with a Taylor Swift outfit complete with tall, western-style boots, and a soft lace and chiffon dress.

'Really!' She wrapped her arm around his, turned him around and started weaving away from the noise and the overloaded dance floor.

'Where are we going?' He frowned but didn't pull his arm free from hers. The warmth of his body and the smell of his spicy aftershave made her smile. His frown disappeared.

'Away from this,' she spoke into his ear as the crowd jostled apart, then closed in behind them.

The tall metal-clad shed was cavernous – large enough to be an aircraft hangar. The smell of hot flesh, hay and machinery lingered. Pushing a side door open, Jenny gulped a lung full of fresh air and embraced the cool desert sky.

'God, I hate crowds.' She let the door close behind Nick. The noise and smell dissipated.

'I'm not a fan myself.' Nick leant against the outside of the galvanized sheeting, watching her every move.

'How's the shoulder?' Jenny stepped closer and patted his arm gently. He wasn't wearing his sling. She hoped the surgery and physio might finally have put him right after the gunshot shattered his shoulder and tore his collarbone apart. The image of him bleeding out on Ken Murphy's polished kitchen floor made her stomach knot. 'You know you should have stayed in the helicopter.'

'You said you'd radio back within five minutes. You didn't.' Nick sounded mildly defensive. 'Besides, that woman had a rifle trained on you when I came in, so I'm pretty glad I didn't listen to you.'

'Me too, except for the fact you got shot of course.' Jenny shouldn't have let Nick use his chopper to help the police – to help her. But she did.

'I'd do it again.' He pushed off the tin shed, turning and stepping in close, pinning her against the metal wall with his eyes.

'That's a scary thought, please don't.' Jenny gazed up at the stars, away from his intense stare. There were millions of tiny glittering lights in the sky out here. She knew they were always there, but out in the desert, they were so visible, so vibrant.

Nick's gaze followed her line of sight, then he turned back to her, his breath soft on her face. His lips inches from hers. She tilted her face toward his, wondering what it would be like to finally kiss him.

A scream erupted, breaking the moment. The tone went from a scream to a shrill, banshee wail.

The hairs on the back of Jenny's neck rose as the cry reached a new note. Nick spun away from her and they chased down the sound with their eyes. A ball of fire ran into view. It dropped to the ground, the scream dying away as flames engulfed fabric. The smell of burning hair made Jenny's nostrils flare.

Nick pulled off his leather jacket and ran toward the flames before Jenny could stop him.

'Call an ambulance!' He wrapped the flames in his coat as voices murmured behind her. A crowd of people emerged from the shed, Nev at the front. His eyes grew wide, before he raced past Jenny toward the victim.

'Call the ambulance!' he yelled at her on his way to help Nick. Why was she rooted to the spot? The dying scream made her blood run cold.

The jostling crowd behind her pushed forward. Someone bumped into her, nudging her from her shock. She reached into her purse, pulled out her phone and dialled as the screams finally stopped. Deep down Jenny knew that wasn't a good sign.

Chapter 2

Jenny focussed on the stars, trying to get the image out of her head. The night was warm, but she stifled a shudder. Cold sweat soaked the back of her dress.

Everything happened so fast. Nick never hesitated. He smothered the fire engulfing the young woman, but it wasn't going to be enough to save her. She knew it wasn't.

The smell of burnt flesh hung in the air as Nev took charge. Being the senior doctor, he rode in the back of the ambulance alongside the patient. Their roommate and paramedic Tim held an IV of fluid which he handed to Nev before securing the gurney ready for transport.

Clear plastic wrap covered the victim's body, along with a sheet to keep her wounds hidden from the amassing crowd of onlookers. But Jenny couldn't get the picture of the scorched victim out of her head. The charred hair, shrivelled flesh, puckered and pitted like a volcanic eruption. The woman's face was unrecognisable.

Her whole body was numb as she watched Tim slam the rear doors, then jump into the driver's seat of the ambulance and pull away. Emily, his partner stayed to attend to Nick. Taking slow, deep breaths she fought to compose herself. This was a crime-scene now. No one caught alight like that by accident. Approaching Nick, she forced a gentle smile.

'You have a habit of playing hero Mr Johnston, don't you?' He shrugged shyly, then grimaced as Emily secured the gauze bandage on his right hand. 'You should go to the hospital.'

'I'm fine.'

Jenny rolled her eyes and turned to the paramedic. 'Should he go to the hospital Emily?' The paramedic smiled knowingly. 'The guys around here aren't big on getting help, but no, Nick was pretty lucky. His wound is a second-degree burn. You'll need to come in and get those dressings changed though. Secondary infection from the blistering is common. And don't forget to take some painkillers if you need them.' She waved her finger at him like a school teacher. He nodded solemnly.

'I've got interviews to do.' Jenny squeezed Nick's unburnt hand. 'Philips and O'Connell are on their way, but I need to take your statement. You were the first to see her.' Another nod from Nick told her to go on. She let his hand go, wishing someone else could do this, but knowing no one was available and a fresh statement was the best statement.

Jenny pulled out her mobile phone, opened the notepad app and studied Nick carefully before continuing. She drew a calming breath, then began. 'Where did you see her come from?'

'Around the corner of that truck over there.' Jenny glanced where he was pointing. Then her eyes focussed back on her notes.

'She was already on fire.' It wasn't a question, but Nick nodded. 'I saw her just after you. I saw you use your coat to put her out. Is there anything you can tell me I might not have seen?'

'Diesel. I could smell diesel.' Nick's nose twitched.

'You think someone used accelerant to set her alight?' Nick nodded again. His eyes remained staring at the charred ground where the victim dropped. His face mirrored the turmoil in her gut. Who on earth sets a young woman on fire? A sick bastard, that's who.

Out the corner of her eyes, she noticed two police four-wheel drives approaching, no lights or sirens. They pulled up alongside one another, and a few seconds later, a truck load of Country Fire Service volunteers arrived. The crew of six climbed down from the vehicle. Their yellow overalls and white fire hats were clean.

'Thanks Nick. I need to get a few more statements.' Jenny turned to meet up with her team, but Nick reached for her arm, gently preventing her from moving away.

'Be careful. Okay?' It was her turn to nod. 'I mean it. Any sicko willing to set someone alight won't have an off switch.' She gazed into his eyes a moment, before patting his hand, still resting on her forearm. The sensation made her want to wrap her arms around him, but Emily was right there, packing away her first-aid equipment.

'I'm already ahead of you.' She glanced at Emily. 'Can you make sure he gets home?' Emily's grin was too accommodating. Visions of the paramedic licking Nick's wounds popped into her head. Her gaze fell back on Nick.

'I've finally found myself a set of wheels. I'll try and come out to see you tomorrow or Sunday.' She challenged Emily with a quick glance. The woman nodded. Unspoken boundaries were set, but as Nick's hand dropped away, she wished she was taking him home tonight.

'Okay.' Still a man of few words. She smiled, which seemed wrong under the circumstances. Turning, she resisted the urge to jog over to Philips, her mind quickly back on her work. There were a few hundred people to interview. It was going to be an excruciatingly long night. She sucked in a breath, shook her shoulders out and mentally prepared herself.

'Hey. This sucks. Puts a dampener on the night.' Philips slammed the Police Landcruiser door shut.

'I think it might suck more for the victim.'

Philips scratched his ear. 'Yeah. Sorry, that was in pretty bad taste. Do we have an ID yet?' 'No. Everything on her was burnt to a crisp.' Jenny's limbs were heavy, as though she were moving underwater.

'First on scene?'

Philips was all business. She wondered if he would be the same if he had seen the screaming victim running right at him? She gathered her thoughts before answering.

'Me and Nick, then Nev who went with her to the hospital.' She glanced over her shoulder at the milling crowd. 'I can't tell you who was next, but all these people could have seen something,' she nodded with her head.

'I'll need to take your statement.'

O'Connell stepped up alongside Constable Philips. 'Let's canvas this lot first, see if anyone knew the victim. We'll conduct a quick search in case there are any obvious signs this was intentional and don't make a mess. A forensic team is on the way.'

'Yes Sir.' Jenny fought the queasiness, the urge to heave. She owed it to the victim though, to find out what the hell happened.

'Philips, you get a hold of, and catalogue every mobile phone here.' O'Connell waved his hand toward the bystanders.

'Sir, Nick saw her come from over there?' She pointed to an enclosed truck. The side was painted with a name in bold blue letters arched over a cattle yard scene with a cowboy playing an acoustic guitar, sitting on the timber railing.

'You okay to secure the scene?' O'Connell studied her. She nodded. He pulled a pair of police issue gloves from his back pocket. 'Try not to mess up that pretty little dress while you're at it.'

Jenny looked down, her cheeks flushed. The off-the-shoulder peasant dress featured a ruffled hem, tight bodice and a burnt-orange and olive paisley pattern that belonged in the sixties.

The jest lightened her mood. 'I can't believe Nev talked me into coming to this show.' She pulled the gloves on, wishing her uniform was in the car where she usually left it.

'Lucky he did. If you hadn't come, these people could have all cleared off.' He waved at the myriad of vehicles parked around the venue, most with mattresses or swags on hand for a long night on the drink. 'At least now we have a ton of possible witnesses. Let's get to it.'

Jenny strode toward the truck. As she approached, the smell of diesel grew stronger. Retrieving her phone, she turned on the torch app and scanned the area – missing her utility vest and high-powered beam. Dark droplets of fluid began at the double doors towards the rear of the truck and trailed around the vehicle out of sight.

She knelt to pinch the red sand with her thumb and fingers, before drawing it to her nose to sniff it. Yep, diesel. Headlights from the C.F.S. appliance struck something under the truck. It glimmered from behind the rear wheel. 'What have we got here?'

Turning her phone torch toward the area revealed a small purple clutch bag with a long silver chain, wedged behind the double rear tyres. Reaching down, she tried to recover it by the chain. Her fingers clawed, she found nothing but dirt.

Straightening up, she glanced around for something to help retrieve it. Her phone torch beam struggled to illuminate more than a few metres into the darkness. She gazed down at her bare knees. Shaking her head, she discounted crawling under the truck, turned her torch light off and rushed back to the police vehicle.

Reaching into the back, she found a police flashlight, a handful of evidence markers and a police-issue baton.

'What's up?' Philips glanced up from his interview.

'I just need to get a few photos. I've found something of interest.' He waved and nodded, his eyes back on the young woman with bright pink hair and a nose ring who chewed gum through every word.

Jenny glanced at her watch, and sighed wondering if she would get any sleep tonight as she flicked the torch on. The brighter beam guided her back to the truck, back to the wheels and purse.

Studying the ground, she tried to retrace her own footprints to preserve the scene. Instead of one set, she found two sets of boot prints near the truck wheel. A rattle near the cab of the truck made her jump, flicking the torch up, she searched for the source.

Her neck muscles tensed, her pulse raced. She was out of uniform and without a weapon. Feeling naked, she wondered if she should call for back-up, but as a small shape bounced into the light beam, turned, bared its teeth, hissed and ran off at speed, she relaxed. Letting out a nervous giggle, she drew a slow breath and stepped back toward the truck wheel.

Using the torch, she peered under the back-double tyre. Ready to push the baton in, she froze. Empty space greeted her. All she could think about was how she missed a chance to photograph the purse. Now it was too late. It was gone.

Chapter 3

'Philips!' she yelled.

Whoever stole the purse couldn't be too far away, but was it worth contaminating the scene to try and find them? 'Shit!' She hated being helpless. Puffing out her cheeks, she turned to see Philips rushing around the corner, Taser in hand.

'What's up?' Philips slowed to a stop, his eyes scanning the area. 'You okay?'

She was still leaning under the truck, desperate to make sure she wasn't seeing things. A void, and scrape marks on the ground confirmed the purse was there before but gone now.

'Did you see anyone come out from here?'

'No. But I was busy with interviews. What's going on?'

She pointed under the truck. Philips scrunched his face, his Taser still at the ready.

'There was a purple clutch under here a minute ago. I went to get evidence markers, a torch and something long enough to reach it but when I got back, it was gone. I was only at the vehicle for a minute, two tops.'

'This place is crawling with people. It could have been anyone.'

'I'll mark up the spot, take a photo of where it was and the footprints around it anyway.'

Philips put his Taser away and Jenny snapped photos on her phone. He peered into the darkness as she worked, waiting to make sure whoever stole the purse didn't come back.

'I'm done.' Let's get back to the interviews.' They rounded the corner of the truck. The crowd was growing restless now the shock and entertainment value was wearing off. 'I want to make sure that truck doesn't leave and no one else gets close to it. I'll be over to join you in a second. I'll ask the C.F.S. guys to keep an eye out.' Philips nodded. Jenny changed direction, striding toward a group of men in yellow overalls and long black boots, their arms across their chests as they waited for instructions.

'Hey guys.' They glanced up. 'I'm Constable Williams. Sorry, out of uniform.' A broad, plump, red-bearded man in his late thirties, with a beer belly that stretched his overall buttons, chuckled as he studied her from top to toe. 'I know. It's hard to take anyone seriously dressed like this. It wasn't my idea. I promise.'

The boots were Nev's idea. He assured her no one went to a BnS without proper footwear.

'Can one of your crew please head over to that truck and tape the area off? Don't walk around the vehicle whatever you do. Just make a perimeter. No one in, no one out. Okay!'

'On it Constable,' red-beard winked.

'Thanks. A forensic team won't be here until – she glanced at her watch and smiled – later today, but if you can keep an eye on it until we've cleared the scene, we'd appreciate it.'

'We can do that.'

'Thanks.'

The Coober Pedy Police consisted of four permanent officers. A case like this stretched them way too thin. Jenny peered toward the East, noting the greyish pre-dawn light before jogging back to the crowd. Her feet ached in the dress boots, but she ignored it, joining Philips and O'Connell, still hard at work collecting phones amongst disgruntled comments.

'All you need to do is rock up at the station tomorrow after you've slept off the grog. Open it up, show us the photos and then you can have it back.' O'Connell was explaining to an inebriated man at least six inches taller than him. For a split second, the situation was ready to escalate, but the man's mate intervened.

'I'll bring him in later.' The man tapped his friend on the shoulder. 'Come on Paul, let's hit the swags for the night eh?' The two men held each other up as they swayed towards a tray-top ute, rigged up for some serious 'roo shooting. The top roll-bar was loaded with various sized spotlights and the UHF aerial was tall enough to make even the cops envious.

'Any luck?' Jenny stepped up alongside O'Connell.

'Most of them have let me flick through the photos here, but we'll still need to download them at the station. I've not seen anything out of the ordinary so far. A few fights caught on video, but none involving a girl who fits our victim's size and height.'

'It's probably a bit late, but I was just about to photograph a piece of evidence – a purple clutch bag with a silver chain from under the band's truck out the back. If you see a photo with a girl and that bag, then she might be our vic.'

'You said just about?' O'Connell stopped scanning a phone, handed it to Philips to record the owner's details and focussed on Jenny.

'Yeah, I went to get a better torch and something long enough to reach under the truck to get it. I should have gotten down on my hands and knees and photographed it then and there, but when I got back, it was gone.'

'You did the right thing. You needed to record the evidence properly or it wouldn't be admissible in court anyway. Did you see anyone?'

'No, just an extra set of boot prints and a nasty feral cat.'

O'Connell chuckled. 'Let's finish up here and interview the band. Then you need to get home and catch some sleep before coming in to work.'

She rolled her eyes. 'I'll be fine. Honest. I'll head backstage now and make sure none of them leave. I've put one of the C.F.S. guys on the truck and asked them to keep the scene secure until all the evidence is collected and we clear the site.'

'Good work Williams. But remember, this isn't a one woman show.' He studied her a moment, waiting for her to read between the lines.

She knew she should get some rest. She was also learning to be a team player, but it was hard. Wanting to be part of a team and giving up control to others were two very different things. The job was only one part of that struggle. Finding her missing cousin and aunt was the other part. Was it time to ask for help?

'Got it.' Jenny forced a smile, then turned to weave her way through the thinning crowd as the sun peaked over the horizon. The sky was clear, not a cloud in sight, which made the pre-dawn temperature crisp. But a clear sky promised a sunny, hot desert day ahead and nowhere was hotter than the red and white sands of the barren Coober Pedy mining fields.

The hangar was empty, except for piles of hay bales and a wall of speakers standing stoically either side of a deadly quiet stage. Bright lights shone down on music equipment left strewn all over the ground. Where are the roadies? Anyone could have strolled in and taken whatever they wanted and no one would even know.

She trudged up the stairs to the left of the stage. Her skin tingled as though she were being watched. Two men tussled in the stage wing – goose bumps covered her body as she wondered what was going on. Her cheeks flushed a moment, before she realised the scene wasn't what she first thought it was.

What appeared at first to be two men, embracing in a passionate kiss turned out to be an exchange of blows, in eerie silence.

'You two. Break it up.' The men ignored her. Shaking her head, she realised the issue was likely her lack of uniform. 'I might not look like it guys, but I'm a cop, so break it up or we can take this down to the station.'

She drew closer, recognising the lead singer and the drummer of the band playing on stage before she'd left the hot, sweaty dance floor.

'Jake Masters right?' The two men finally followed her instruction. 'Like I said, I'm a cop. We need to talk.' She didn't know the name of the drummer, but the lead singer was plastered all over the BnS advertising material including the truck outside. The poster child so to speak – was a good-looking guy who seemed fully aware of his charm.

'That's right honey.' His smarmy smile made her sneer reflexively. He was the type of guy who was sexist, but thought he was charismatic.

'I might not be in uniform mate, but if you call me honey again, I'll arrest you, just for that.'

'You can't.' He looked unsure.

'I can call it refusing to cooperate with an officer.' She shrugged. 'Or you two can help me find the rest of your crew and we can have that chat I suggested.'

They exchanged a glance. A silent question passed between them before they returned her scrutinising gaze.

'What were you fighting about?' Jenny watched their body language carefully. Something wasn't right about this scene but she hadn't put her finger on it yet.

'Nothing important.' Jake shrugged a little too casually.

'It was important enough to lay into each other.' She waited, hands on hips anticipating the lame lie she knew was coming.

'Just band stuff,' drummer boy answered. It was all she was going to get right now. Was it linked to her case? Possibly, but now wasn't the time to dig into it.

'Speaking about the band. Where are the rest of them?' She waved her hand toward the backstage area, not bothering to hide her frustration.

'How should I know where they are?' Jake crossed his arms defiantly over his chest.

'Well your truck is still parked out back.' They glanced at one another, then averted their gaze. 'And your roadies haven't started packing your gear yet?'

They laughed. 'We don't have roadies,' Jake scoffed.

'Okay, well you and your crew haven't started packing up. So the rest of the band have to be here somewhere.'

'We've been occupied. We aren't due in Emerald until next Thursday, so we were enjoying the local talent.'

'So you've been shagging a few locals but you dragged yourself away to have a little fight?

I find that hard to believe.'

'Look!' Jake puffed out his chest. 'What's all this about anyway?'

Jenny shook her head, amazed they could have missed the night's earlier events. 'A girl was set on fire outside earlier this evening.' They gaped at her, then glanced at each other again. 'Where the hell have you two been? Why do you think the crowd ran outside? You must have heard the ambulance arrive?'

'Ambulances aren't anything new at these gigs.' The drummer seemed to believe that explained everything.

'And you get a mass exodus from your gigs often? I didn't think you were that bad.' Jenny played along.

'Ha ha.' Jake scowled. 'We get paid either way. We knew something dragged them all outside. It's usually a brawl,' he shrugged. 'But honestly, I couldn't give a rat's bum what the issue was. I took a smoke, drank a beer, fell asleep, woke up, Curtis here was shagging my ride. We fought, then you came in.'

It sounded plausible, but there was something about Jake's manner suggesting that wasn't the whole story.

'Your ride didn't happen to have a purple purse with a long silver chain on her?'

Chapter 4

Jenny was exhausted. Every nerve in her body was shot. Even Nikolic's real bean caramel latte wasn't making up for less than three hours of sleep. At least a shower and clean uniform were going halfway to making her feel human again.

'We ready to start these interviews?' Jenny opened the countertop and dragged herself toward the bay of lockers next to O'Connell's desk.

'You look terrible.' Philips grinned.

'You don't exactly look like Captain America yourself.'

'Sarge wants a report and we still don't have your statement Williams. We'll start in the Boss's office with both.' O'Connell tapped keys on his computer, his eyes not leaving the screen.

Jenny sighed. Her relationship with her commanding officer was far from perfect. Despite her saving his skin twice now, the guy liked to keep her on a short leash. At first, she thought he was a chauvinistic old-school cop, but she now understood his daughter's death made him over-protective.

The fact she sniffed out cases more thoroughly than her predecessor Senior Constable Len Holmes, didn't seem to sway Sergeant Mackenzie entirely, but at least now he was beginning to trust her instincts.

'Can I at least finish this before I face that?' She lifted her coffee cup in the direction of the Boss's closed door.

'You've got two minutes. We need to wait for the band's lawyer to arrive in any case.' O'Connell finally peered over the top of his reading glasses.

'Lawyer. That's ominous.'

'It certainly says they've got something to hide, but it could have nothing to do with our victim.' O'Connell returned his gaze to the keyboard.

'How's she doing?' Jenny sipped her coffee.

'DOA.' Senior Constable O'Connell glanced up at her silence, studying her closely. 'Sorry. I thought you knew already.'

She shook her head. 'So it's murder?' It shouldn't have been a shock, but her arms went limp as she lifted her coffee to her lips. Swallowing grew difficult.

'We don't know that until forensics gets into it. Your mate should be here any minute.'

'Who's picking her up?' Jenny's adrenalin picked up. Suddenly wide awake. Penny was more than a forensic scientist. She was one of the few people Jenny counted as a friend.

'Nev agreed to. She wanted to see the body first up.'

Jenny sighed, sipped her coffee, savouring the last few mouthfuls before having to relive the incident again for her statement. 'That's one part of Penny's job I really don't envy.'

'None of us do, but the chick's got balls. She doesn't shy away from any of it.' Philips smiled proudly. Even though Penny McGregor had no link to Philips or Coober Pedy, the town recently adopted her as their own.

Since moving there in January, Jenny dealt with three murders or suspicious death cases including this latest. The opal mining town was known for domestic violence, accidental deaths and even drugs, but three major crimes in three months was unheard of.

Philips often joked she was a murder magnet, and right now, Jenny was beginning to believe it. She hoped it didn't extend to her missing cousin and aunt.

Tossing her coffee cup in the bin, she shook herself out of her melancholy. 'Let's get this statement over with. Then we can talk strategy with these band boys. Something doesn't sit right with their stories.'

Jenny sauntered to Sergeant Mackenzie's office, stopped before the door, drew a slow, steady breath, then knocked.

'It's open.' Pushing the door fully open, she entered. 'You wanted a report Sir.'

'I'll come out.' Sarge pushed his high-backed office chair away from the desk and stood slowly, his serious gaze sadder than usual. Losing his daughter in an horrific car accident cost him his marriage and nearly his career. The depths of drunken depression swallowed him up. It was all before her time, but the boys claimed he was all good these days.

'Tough night Williams.' She nodded. 'You should talk to someone.' She could see he wasn't offering to be that someone. 'O'Connell maybe?'

'Going over it again for my statement will be enough,' she assured him. He studied her a moment until she squirmed. Who was she trying to convince? Him or her?

He cleared his throat, then stepped past her out into the main office. 'Okay team. Where are we at? Let's start from the top Williams. Tell us how it unfolded.' He sat on the edge of O'Connell's desk.

'I don't know if seeing it first-hand will be any help, but...' She let the rest trail away as she composed herself, fighting back memories of a high-pitched scream. She stifled a shiver.

Explaining where she was, what she saw, how Nick took charge, how the girl slumped to the ground, increased her anxiety level. Her earlier hot shower cleaned her skin, but nothing could wash the smell of burning flesh from her nostrils.

'Nasty.' Philips gagged.

'We need to catch the bastard.' Sarge's temple vein pulsed.

'First we better work out who she is.' O'Connell tapped keys on his computer. 'No one has reported anyone missing yet.'

'So none of our witnesses came forward to say their friend didn't come home with them and still hasn't turned up?' Jenny shook her head, mumbling silently to herself. She always buddied up when partying in Adelaide.

'It was a BnS. It could take another twenty-four hours before anyone works out who went home with who, or who is still recovering under a ute somewhere outside the venue.'

'Reckless,' Sarge grumbled and Jenny agreed with him.

'You would have been as loose when you were young.' O'Connell sounded confident, but Jenny wasn't so sure.

'Maybe it's a female thing, but you don't leave your friends behind. It's so stupid.'

'Stupid it might be, but it's more common than you think. Date rape is the most unreported crime. Maybe the victims believe their decisions contributed to the rape so they don't tell anyone, but they should. We can't catch them if we don't know.' Philips rattled off the statistics so easily, making Jenny wonder if he knew someone who was a victim of date rape.

'Well, we don't know if date rape has anything to do with this case. Could be a disgruntled boyfriend. Burning a victim is nearly always personal and power related.' Jenny shared her opinion.

'Like rape.' Philips returned to the subject. It was possible, but it wasn't their only avenue of enquiry.

'Either way, rape and/or murder, we need to get this predator before he decides to get upset with another innocent victim.' The Sergeant pushed to his feet, ready to return to his office but stopped. Gazing back over his shoulder, his eyes rested on Jenny. 'You be bloody careful Williams. Whoever stole the purse from the scene likely knows who you are now.'

'I'll be careful Sir.'

'No showboating.' He shook his finger at her. 'You find something on this one, even a little clue, you bring it to me. I don't want you unravelling this case behind the scenes like your last two big cases. You understand!'

'Yes Sir.' She was expecting this lecture, but for the first time is was being delivered without an accusation of ulterior motives.

'Keep us in the loop Williams.' He scuttled back to his office and closed the door. 'He's right you know.' Philips added his two cents' worth.

'I know. I get it, but these cases mull around in my head and it's like a lightbulb moment. I don't know I'm going to join the dots until they're joined and then it's too late to let you know. It's not like there was mobile reception last time and my UHF radio had limited range.'

The mentally unstable pageant mother who abused her daughter, then hunted down the guy who sheltered her with the delusion he murdered her, was the weirdest case Jenny ever heard of. Something out of a Hollywood movie plot.

She could still see Suzanna Thompson waving her gun around with every intention of using it. Jenny didn't put all the pieces together until she was standing right there in front of the woman – right in the line of fire, but it was Nick who took the bullet. When she turned around to see blood pumping from his chest, her heart leapt into her throat exactly like it was now. O'Connell spoke, pulling her back to the present.

'Well, to help keep the pieces on the table we'll run a murder board in the station. You put everything you think is linked to the case on it.' O'Connell wheeled a whiteboard out from the back room. 'Got it!'

'Why are we handling this and not a detective anyway?' Jenny knew there was no point asking the question, but it was her way of covering her butt if anything went south in the future. No one could say she didn't recommend passing the case over.

Coober Pedy didn't have a resident detective. Major crimes usually required a city detective to be called in. So far, her boss failed to do so on any of the recent major crime's cases. Each time he preferred not to upset the locals and handle it in-house. No one ever challenged Sarge, until she came to town.

If they'd called in a detective for Nick's dad's death, then maybe she wouldn't be chasing her tail trying to confirm if it was suicide or not. Now, she braced herself for the answer she knew was coming.

'Until forensics confirm it's murder, we'll deal with a death by misadventure.' O'Connell pulled a whiteboard marker from his top desk drawer and began writing.

'I hate that term. Setting yourself alight is highly unlikely to have been a misadventure.'

'We'll know more once Penny does her thing.' Philips sounded confident.

The sound of someone clearing their throat made the entire team turn toward the front counter in unison. A tall, thin, long-legged brunette in an expensive business suit waited at reception. The sound of her wedge-heeled foot tapping impatiently echoed on the worn linoleum floor.

'I'd like to see my clients now.'

Chapter 5

Jenny glanced at her watch for the twentieth time. The country band's lead singer Jake and drummer Curtis were crammed in one interview room with two other band members she didn't know yet and their lawyer.

It wasn't wise, in her opinion, to let them get their stories straight before being interviewed, but letting them all see their lawyer individually could have taken all day. So far, there was nothing concrete to even connect them to the victim, other than Jake's expression when she mentioned the purple purse.

The interview door opened with a creak. Samantha Haynes stepped out with the confidence of someone more accustomed to working with fashion icons or high-end business people than this little country rock band. Jenny knew appearances could be deceiving. An extensive check on the lawyer while she conferred with her clients revealed some interesting information.

'We are ready for you now officers.' Her posh accent made Jenny's hair stand on end. Her file said she grew up in country Victoria, went to private boarding school in Melbourne, studied at the university of Melbourne and must have slept with someone at the top of the food chain to make junior partner in the third largest law firm in Melbourne in only six short years.

She knew she was being sexist. The woman could have an IQ of a thousand for all she knew, but something about the sky-rocketing female lawyer's career didn't ring true.

'You've got this one Williams.' O'Connell pointed to Philips. 'You can ride shotgun.' The lawyer smiled confidently. She likely thought it was a windfall dealing with two raw junior constables. 'Let's take them one at a time though.' The arrogant smile disappeared with the realisation it was going to be a long day.

Jenny couldn't hold back a grin as she entered the interview room. 'Boys, let's start with Jake. You three, follow Constable Philips to the front office. Behave yourselves and we won't have to lock you in our tiny holding cells while you wait.'

Jake sat back, folded his arms and straightened his legs to press his crotch forward in true alpha style. Jenny scoffed as chairs scraped back, and the other three band members shuffled out.

'Can I have a glass of water?' He rubbed his throat with his hand and winced. 'I have to keep my voice for our next gig.'

'I heard your performance last night,' she tutted, 'not sure water will help.' She was surprised to hear the lawyer chuckle as she held the door for her clients to leave.

Jake faltered for a split second, before a condescending smirk returned. 'Let's get the recording sorted.' Jenny fiddled with the equipment.

'You haven't read me my rights.' It was Jenny's turn to chuckle.

'Mate, you're not under arrest. You are simply helping us with our enquiries.' He gaped at his lawyer as she lowered herself delicately into the seat alongside him.

'So I don't have to be here?' He pushed up from his chair. Hayes put her hand on his shoulder and pulled him back down into his seat.

'We'll do the police a courtesy, then you can be on your way Jake.'

There was no doubt the lawyer was in charge. Why? Who was she to him?

Philips returned, shuffled into a seat alongside Jenny and nodded as he pressed the button on the recording equipment.

'Please state your full name and date of birth for the recording.'

Jake rolled his eyes, leant back to take up his earlier position and sighed. 'Jake Masters, eighteen Feb, nineteen ninety. When can we move our truck? We usually live in it.'

'It will need to stay where it is for now. We need time to finish our forensic investigation.'

His lawyer gave him a sideways glance. Was it a warning to stick to answering the questions or was it something else?

'Jake, you gave me the impression you saw a woman with a purple clutch purse at the BnS ball last night.'

'I saw a lot of women last night.' He winked. She sneered.

'This particular woman, was burned alive last night, so let's try and be a little empathetic, shall we?'

He cleared his throat, finally gauging the temperature of the room. 'Yeah, the chick...'

'Young woman or lady might be the word you're looking for.' Jenny didn't know why, but he was aggravating her. Hayes smiled again.

'She was no lady.' Jake lunged forward so rapidly that Philips moved into a defensive position. Jenny put her hand on his forearm.

'So you did speak with her?'

'I didn't say that.' Hayes leant over and whispered into his ear. His brow creased. His eyes opened wide. The lawyer's face was set firm. She nodded toward Jenny.

'Okay. I knew her.' He slumped back in his seat, arms over his chest.

'Knew her, like you hooked up with her or you knew her?'

'Melinda Smart.' A name. That was freaking awesome, but how did Jake know her?

'You have history then?' Jenny watched Philips taking notes. He glanced at her a second, his eyes saying what she was thinking.

'I've known Melinda since we were ten.' An age too. Now they were getting somewhere.

'Dated?'

'In high school, yeah. But haven't seen her for years, not since she went off to university and I went on the road.'

'Was the reunion amicable?'

'I saw her. I fobbed her off.' Jake looked at his hands. 'Now she's dead.' His shoulders sagged.

He liked her.

'Why did you stop dating in high school?'

Jake's nostrils flared as he sucked in air. 'Her dad.' The statement was so matter of fact, as though Jenny should already know the answer. The penny dropped. Samantha Hayes was junior partner in a firm. The name on the computer screen flashed like a neon sign in Jenny's mind.

Campbell, Newman and Smart.

Chapter 6

Jenny couldn't wait to push through the remaining interviews. Her head was reeling with information. Why would their victim's father send their junior partner to oversee the band's interviews? And why did said lawyer tell her client to admit to the relationship?

Curtis was an interesting one. The guy didn't have the alpha streak, in fact, he could have been described as the complete opposite.

'I didn't go to school with Jake. We met at the Tamworth Music Festival.' He didn't make eye contact with Samantha Hayes. The lawyer sat back in her chair, listening to the interview without objection.

'You were there as spectators?'

'No. We were fresh out of high school. The festival was running an amateur competition. I answered a drummer advert Jake posted.'

'When was this?'

'Two thousand and eight, late November.' Jenny checked Philips was taking notes for quick reference later. He glanced up and nodded.

'But you didn't meet until the festival. That's in January?'

Curtis's eyebrows rose at her knowledge, but he carried on without comment.

'Jake's a huge YouTuber. He has a massive following, going way back to early two thousand and eight, when hardly anyone except school aged kids knew what YouTube even was.'

Jenny nodded for him to go on.

'I heard him sing. He's raw. He was even more so back then, but hell he sings with passion and that's what country music is all about.' Jenny watched Curtis's face light up.

'So how did he choose you to be in the band?'

'I recorded a CD, sent it to him. He phoned. We talked and met up a few days before the festival to practise with the other band members he chose.'

'So Jake put the band together?'

Curtis nodded, then sat back in the chair. 'And we all grabbed his tail feathers. From YouTube to live gigs like here.'

'And you never met Melinda Smart before this weekend?'

Curtis shook his head. 'I didn't meet her even then. I saw her with Jake before he crashed out.'

'Melinda wasn't his ride you stole?'

Curtis scoffed. 'We weren't fighting over any girl.'

'What were you fighting about?'

Curtis leant forward, his elbows leaning on the interview desk. 'I'm leaving the band and he wasn't happy about it.'

It didn't seem relevant, but Hayes must have thought it was. She leant forward and subtly tapped his arm. He looked sideways at her. The shake of her head was gentle, but obvious. Curtis sat back and sucked in a frustrated breath.

'Can I go now? I need to pack. I've got to get back to Brisbane.'

'Look, a girl has been viciously murdered. We need to go through a ton of video footage from the evening. It's spread out over about two hundred mobile phones. Once we've seen all the footage, you can leave, but not before.'

'We record every gig. If I get you last night's recording, showing we were all still on stage when this happened, can we leave?'

Jenny glanced at Philips, who shrugged. If they were all playing when she witnessed Melinda's murder, then there would be no reason to keep them. The thought disappointed her because if the band members were all in the clear, their suspect pool would be so much bigger.

'If you can provide the video, if it shows you all on stage, and if you leave a forwarding address and contact details where we can call and confirm before you leave, then and only then can we consider letting you leave.'

'I'll get it sorted.'

There was a moment of silence as Jenny studied Curtis's face. His long thin nose, sharp jaw, blue eyes and cowlick made him look like a genuine country rock movie star, but he wasn't like Jake. His expression was earnest. His manner genuine, even humble. Was it an act?

'We'll finish our interviews, you get the recording organised. Then we'll confirm with our Sergeant. If it all pans out, you can leave on the early flight tomorrow.' She pushed her chair back to leave then indicated for Philips to stop the recording.

'What's so urgent in Brisbane?'

'My sister's having a baby.' The answer came too quickly. Jenny studied Curtis a moment. He didn't cringe at the scrutiny. Maybe he was just excited?

Chapter 7

Jenny tied her long auburn ponytail into a tight bun, her stomach grumbled loudly.

O'Connell glanced up, a curve of his lips confirmed he heard her hunger pangs. 'The interviews are done. You should grab a bite to eat.'

'Coffee girl's here.' Penny held a tray aloft as she danced into the main office.

'Your timing is impeccable.' Jenny controlled her urge to jump up and give Penny a massive hug. Instead, she waited patiently until Penny held out the tray, then she lifted the coffee marked with a J inside a heart.

'Sir,' Penny gently put O'Connell's coffee on his desk, 'I need to process the crime scene. Can I grab your ride and head out there now?'

'Sure. You done with the victim?'

'I am. She is on her way to Doc for an autopsy. I've gathered as much evidence as I could. I've sent the samples with the body for processing.'

'Do you have a preliminary report?'

'Only what you already guessed. The accelerant was common diesel. The girl suffered third degree burns to over eighty percent of her body. The average human won't live with anything over fifty percent. She didn't have a chance.'

Jenny's stomach clenched, the smell of burning flesh still vivid. O'Connell sighed, closed his eyes and sipped his coffee. Jenny wondered if he was relaxing with the good coffee or was he trying not to think about what a body covered in eighty percent burns looked like? Jenny wished she was blissfully unaware.

'Take Williams with you. The keys are up there.' He pointed to a hook on the pegboard next to the lockers.

'I'm supposed to be running background on Smart and his legal firm.' Jenny didn't protest too loudly. She liked the idea of spending the rest of the afternoon on scene with Penny.

'Phillips and I can get started. It's not often a forensic scientist gets to examine a scene with an eyewitness. Besides, whoever nicked the purse could still be lurking around. Two sets of eyes are better than one.'

'Let's go then. Grab your coffee.' Penny was already striding for the door, bags in hand.

'Wait up. I need to get my vest.' Jenny reached into her locker, pulled out her utility vest and waist-belt before locking the door and turning to the weapons cabinet. Signing the register, she checked out her police issue pistol, and smiled at Penny's tapping foot. 'Don't leave home without it.'

'All set?'

'Let's go.'

Twenty minutes later they unloaded Penny's kit on site. 'I'll start at the truck.' Penny bent down and undid one of the cases. 'Where was the purse?'

'Just over here.' Jenny lifted the police tape.

'Hold up. Put these on.' A pair of shoe covers and gloves were shoved in her direction.

'Okay.' Jenny stretched the covers over her boots, then pulled the gloves on before cautiously approaching the rear wheel of the truck. Stopping a metre away, being careful not to disturb the footprints, she turned to Penny. 'Here.'

Penny pulled the lens cover from her digital camera, snapped a few shots, then crouched to study the diesel drops in the red sand.

'I spotted the bag. Went to the truck to grab a better flashlight and evidence markers. When I got back, I heard a noise near the front of the truck. I investigated. Saw a feral cat, but no one else, but when I got back to here, the bag was gone.'

'See this?' Penny hurried to her forensic kit, retrieved an evidence marker then returned to take a photo. 'I'll need to take castings, but I think these are female boot prints. Size seven or eight maybe.'

'I'm a ladies ten.'

'I guessed as much. I'll need a print from your shoes to eliminate, but it looks like someone invaded your scene and took the bag before you could.'

'They must have been pretty confident. I was only gone a minute.'

Penny returned to her forensic kit to mix up a batch of casting stone. 'Lucky you weren't still here. You were unarmed and they were desperate enough to risk exposure.'

'I won't make that mistake again.' She tapped her gun subconsciously as she watched Penny squat and pour a pale-yellow liquid into the footprint. 'The question is, who owned the bag? Our victim or the woman who stole it?'

Penny didn't answer, her eyes were fixed on the boot print. 'Okay, time to check out the truck.'

'What about the boot print?'

'I'll leave it a minute to set, then collect it. You said you heard a noise up the front of the truck. Did you find any boot prints there?'

Penny collected her fingerprinting powder and began spinning the brush over the door surface. She put the brush down, collected a swab kit and touched it on the truck door lever, outside surface and various places, then cut the swab into a vial of reactant.

'No, but the light was pretty crappy on scene before dawn.'

'I think we might have hit the mother lode. The truck lights up for MDMA.' She shook the vial in the air.

'No wonder Jake was in such a hurry to remove it.' Jenny studied the padlock. 'I guess we'll try the nice way first. I'll ask O'Connell to get Hayes to ask her clients if we can have a key. God how I hate dealing with lawyers.'

'Not sure this will be related to the murder though. Didn't you say the band were all on stage when the victim died?'

'They were.'

'So the female footprint might be the key.'

Jenny sighed. 'It could be. But drugs could also be a motive. Did you find any prints on the truck?'

'Lots. It will take me the rest of the day to sort through them back at the station. We'll need the band members' prints, for elimination of course.' Penny grinned mischievously, her eyebrows wiggling. Jenny laughed.

'I'll call O'Connell and ask for the keys and make sure we have the band members' prints.' Jenny pulled her phone out the front pocket of her vest. 'Let me know if you need anything. Reception is crap here, so I'll need to be in range of the car's mobile booster.' Penny didn't answer. Jenny peered at her phone screen, watching the bars flicker between none and one. A few steps from the vehicle, she saw one and a half bars pop onto the screen. It would have to do.

The phone rang for an agonising thirty seconds. Finally, someone picked up. 'Coober Pedy Police, Constable Philips speaking.'

'Philips. It's Williams.' It was funny how they used last names on the job, but Danny was a super nice bloke and his first name suited him. She often stopped herself from using it at work.

'Nice of you to leave me with the admin.'

'Not my call mate. Ask O'Connell.'

He chuckled good-naturedly.

'I need to get the keys to the band's truck.' She explained the MDMA. 'Under the circumstances, we don't need permission, but I figured we better at least give Hayes a courtesy call.'

'You got it. I'll get her to call you directly.'

Jenny hung up, put her phone away and returned to Penny, whose eyes were focussed on pressing tape over black powder and gently transferring prints onto a piece of white card. She grinned. 'Ooh. Look here. Lady's prints.'

'How can you tell?' Jenny leant in close.

'Well, to be honest, I can't. But they are smaller than a fully grown male.' She placed it into an evidence box and continued pulling prints.

'I don't know. Guitarists have super long, skinny fingers and they often grow crazy long nails too.'

Penny turned, eyebrow lifted. 'What? I dated a bass guitarist when I was in the police academy.'

'Oh, speaking of dating. How's things going with Nick?' Penny eyes didn't shift from her work.

'They aren't going anywhere. We talk, but it's always about his family or mine.'

'He's fully into you.'

Jenny wondered if pursuing a relationship with Nick was wise. They were drawn together over their shared family issues, but if Nick's dad turned out to have been involved…

She voiced her fears with Penny as the forensic scientist photographed fingerprints.

'Don't be ridiculous. Nothing ventured, nothing gained. Better to have loved and lost than never to have loved at all – and all that type of stuff. It's true you know.'

Jenny sighed. Deep down she knew it was. So why was she wimping out now? Her mum and dad's relationship was good. It wasn't Hollywood passionate or anything, but it was fine. Then she thought about Uncle Pete and Aunt Carolyn. Had they been close?

Her phone rang. The number was unknown. She answered. 'Constable Williams.'

'Constable,' Jenny sighed loudly. It wasn't who she hoped to speak with today. 'I'm trying to find those keys for you, but they seem to be misplaced.'

Of course they are! 'It was only a courtesy call Ms Hayes. Mr Sullivan is sure to have bolt cutters or a grinder in his shed here.'

'No need to be like that. Give us another fifteen minutes and if we can't find them, then go ahead and break the lock, by all means.'

Jenny frowned. The woman was being far too sweet. 'Fifteen minutes Ms Hayes, then I'm done. We don't have all day to wait for your clients.'

'Of course.'

Jenny supressed a shudder as the lawyer hung up.

'Who was that?' Penny kept her eyes on the ground as she searched the truck perimeter, studying the underside of the vehicle with a torch.

'Hayes. She asked for fifteen minutes to find the keys.' Jenny glanced at her watch. 'She has ten to go.'

'I'd say you have probable cause, so let's break this baby open.' Penny lifted her eyebrows, her eyes glinting, waiting for Jenny to agree.

'I could at least check in the shed and see if there is anything close by we can use. Otherwise, I'll have to call Mr Sullivan which could take more than ten minutes anyway.'

'Sounds like a plan. I'll pack this gear in the Cruiser and get ready to print the inside once it's open.' Penny ducked under the tape with a cardboard box full of evidence.

Jenny approached the smaller shed, next to the large hangar, hoping it held tools. Grabbing the handle, she twisted, smiling when it opened.

Peering into the darkness, she patted around the corner with her hand, searching for a light switch. Finding nothing, she pulled a torch from her utility vest. Flicking it on, she swung the beam to scan the immediate area looking for a switch, even a hanging light. Nothing.

The dust rose from the unsealed floor with each step, floating in the light beam. A crash ahead made her jump back, heart pounding in her chest. Reaching for her Taser, she scanned the piles of machinery, tools and boxes with her torch in her left hand.

Shadows danced in the light beam. Another sound made Jenny spin, flooding the area with torch light. A wooden box rolled, then thudded on the dirt, a puff of dust exploded. Jenny watched the dust settle. Her pulse sounded in her ears. Movement outside the beam of light made her shift erratically. A rat scurried into view, stopping, its nose twitching, before it scuttled away.

She chuckled nervously, her Taser still held at the ready, but her heart rate steadied. Stepping further into the darkness, the torch beam flicked from side to side, taking in the wooden racks full of oil cans, power tools, motor parts and boxes.

Jenny found what she was looking for at the rear of the shed. A long bench covered the entire wall. A pegboard loaded with tools, carefully laid out in size order made finding what she needed so much easier.

A set of bolt cutters longer than her arm hung high on the right-hand side of the tool bench. Grabbing them down, she turned to make her way to the entrance. A glimmer of light showed the way, but with only a few steps to go, the door slammed shut. Jenny thought it was the wind, but when she reached the door and pushed, her heart thudded inside her chest and bile rose in her throat.

'Penny!' she shouted. 'I'm stuck in the shed.' There was no reply. 'Penny!' she yelled louder. She opened her mouth to try one more time, but stopped as a sound like a jet engine warming up on the runway turned into an explosion, throwing her from her feet, through the air to land on her backside, sliding to a stop on the dirt floor.

'Oh God. Penny!'

Chapter 8

Shaking her head, she launched to her feet and ran at the door. Thumping, she called out, 'Penny. Are you okay?' Another smaller explosion sent her pulse racing in her ears. The building shook, boxes tumbled from racks.

The shed was pitch black, except for her flashlight casting an eerie glow on the side wall. Smoke began to filter around the beam of light. Jenny leant against the jammed door, coughing. Behind the door, scorching heat forced her to back away, scanning the roofline as flames licked at the metal around her.

Penny, please don't be anywhere near that explosion! She searched for her mobile phone, retrieving it with shaking hands. She knew reception was unlikely, but it was her only chance. A spasm of coughing racked her body. She dropped to her knees, crawling on the ground trying to avoid the rising smoke.

She punched in the station number, but nothing happened, not even a dial tone. Desperately, she texted Philips in case an SMS could get through. She tried calling again, nothing! Flames rolled along the timber beams overhead. Sweat touched every exposed piece of skin.

Fighting the temptation to remove her utility vest, Jenny drew away from the heat, further away from the door – her only escape. Hunching down like a frightened child at the rear of the shed, she watched helplessly as smoke filled the roofline.

'Stay calm.' She spoke aloud. 'Just keep your head on Williams.' Using a tone O'Connell or Sarge might, she forced herself to slow her breathing down. Smoke drifted down from the ceiling as the sound of voices rose from outside the metal walls.

'She's in there. I know she's in there. I saw her go in.'
'Stay calm Miss.'

'Penny! I'm in here!' Jenny thumped the metal wall, which rattled loudly.

'I know you're bloody in there. I told the farmer you're in there!' Penny couldn't control her anger and frustration. Jenny knew the feeling.

The smoke dropped lower, choking, suffocating as it closed in around her. The heat radiated from every wall now. Jenny sank lower, onto her belly; her face in the dirt as embers dropped to the boxes and stuck.

'The fire is inside!' she yelled, trying desperately to keep the panic from her voice.

'Truck's on the way.' An older male voice spoke through the wall. 'We'll have you out in a jiffy luv.'

'I'm not sure I've got a jiffy,' she called back, her voice soft in her own ears as her world spun out and darkness enveloped her.

****

Jenny opened her eyes to a sea of faces hovering around her. She pulled something from her face and pushed to get up. A firm hand held her down.

'Wait up there Williams.' Sergeant Mackenzie's brow was furrowed, his eyes drilled her with concern.

'I'm fine Sir.'

Her paramedic roommate Tim smiled, then replaced the oxygen mask over her mouth and nose. 'You'll need to come to hospital. Take in a little oxygen. You might be done for today Jenny.'

She ignored him, instead, her eyes focussed on the firefighting team working on the shed and truck across the yard from where the ambulance parked up, back doors still wide open.

'Whatever was in the truck is gone now.' Sarge answered her unasked question.

'Damn!' She pulled the mask away, her eyes darted around, suddenly recalling earlier events. 'Penny. Where's Penny?' She pushed up from the gurney. A hacking cough choked her closing throat. This time she sat back and put the mask on willingly as the inside of the ambulance spun.

'Penny's fine.'

'Yep.' Penny stepped up into the ambulance, making the small space seem oppressive with her tall, broad-shouldered figure blocking out whatever light was coming through the open doors. 'I'm good. Got tossed into the air like a rag doll when the explosion went off, but I was still loading evidence into the police Cruiser when it happened.'

'We still have the prints you lifted. Right?'

'Yes, Philips has taken them back to the station. O'Connell is holding the fort for now.'

'Did we get the band members' prints?'

Sergeant Mackenzie waved his hand around the ambulance. 'This kind of put a halt to proceedings.'

'Was that the intention?' She sat forward. Tim shook his head and drew the back up on the gurney as it became obvious Jenny wasn't going to stay lying down. 'What time did Philips call Hayes?'

'O'Connell called around four thirty. We can confirm from the station phone records if you want. What are you thinking?' Sarge leant forward.

'I'm thinking she didn't call me back until after four fifty, then she asked for another fifteen minutes.'

'You think she was stalling? O'Connell told her you'd be cutting the lock open because there were traces of drug residue on the truck and due to the nature of Meth, we had no choice but to ensure the truck didn't pose a threat.' Sarge glanced up at Penny as he spoke.

'You can say that again. The thing went up like fireworks on Guy Fawkes Day.'

'I told her the same!' A spasm in Jenny's throat stopped her talking. Another round of hacking coughs made her lay back. Tim reached for her hand and clamped a piece of monitoring equipment to her index finger. A screen popped to life with oxygen and pulse rate.

'You're done Jenny. I need to get you to the hospital. Nev will shoot me if your lungs pack up.' He pointed to the monitor, her oxygen saturation was dropping below ninety five percent. She knew that wasn't good.

The coughing continued, tears ran down her cheeks. Nodding agreement, she watched Sarge and Penny back out of the ambulance.

'I'd come with you if I could, but I need to process this new scene.' Penny squeezed her foot gently from the doorway.

'You do that.' Jenny croaked out before another fit of coughing stopped her talking. She waved goodbye between hacking spasms as the ambulance driver slammed the doors and jumped into the driver's seat.

The gurney was lowered flat once more, leaving Jenny staring at the roof of the ambulance wondering what five more minutes in that shed would have meant.

Chapter 9

Jenny trudged into the dugout she shared with Nev and Tim. Her head ached, her feet were heavier than bar bells. Moving out of town to take the boys' third bedroom seemed like a good idea, but tonight, as exhaustion caught up with her she wished she still lived at the Opal Miner's Motel.

It was so convenient, right across the road from the cop station. On nights like tonight the pub was much easier. Order dinner, eat, shower and crash. But too much pub food and the lure of late night drinks wasn't healthy and the former mine, converted to an underground 'country cottage' was like home to her now.

'You look stuffed.' Nev held a beer and a plate of stir-fried chicken he'd saved for her. 'Take a seat.' He nodded to the lounge.

'You don't know how much I need this.' Jenny tossed her backpack on the kitchen bench.

'The beer or the food.' Nev followed her to the plush grey couch.

'Both.' She collapsed into the lounge harder than intended, knocking it backwards a few inches against the wall.

'You okay?' Nev handed her the food, a concerned frown was out of place on the guy who was usually all smiles. 'Tim called.'

'I'm fine.' She sighed. Nev wasn't on duty when she arrived at the hospital, but it was a mistake to think Tim wouldn't tell him.

'I know. I called the doctor on duty. Told him not to let you out unless he was sure you were all good.'

'I should have known. I tried to leave twice and he stopped me.' Nev gave a satisfied grin. 'My oxygen levels are back up above ninety-eight and I told him there was a resident doctor at home.' She grinned. 'Should have known you already talked to him.'

'Tim did the right thing calling me. We both know how pig-headed you can be.' Jenny rolled her eyes. 'Seriously, you weren't getting out of there if the duty doctor didn't give you the all clear. Philips was on standby to handcuff you to the bed.' He grinned. She punched him in the arm gently.

They fell silent. Jenny wasn't hungry, but she scooped up a mouthful and ate anyway. Other than when Melanie went missing, it was probably the worst twenty-four hours of her life.

She wondered what Nev was thinking. She knew he did everything he could to save Melinda but her burns were horrific. Penny said as much. Now it was her job to work out who killed her. It was going to be a tough one. Her chest tightened as the woman's scream filled her memory.

'What a horrible way to die.' Jenny drew a long mouthful of beer, then placed the stubby on the Redgum slab coffee table. The high gloss finish was very eighties, but the timber was real and rugged. It matched the old timber front door and barn style décor.

'I don't think there are many more terrible ways to go.' Nev took a half-hearted sip of his beer. 'If it's any consolation, after the initial burns, she never regained consciousness.'

'That's a blessing for her, but not so great for solving her murder.' She sipped her beer. The silence mounted.

'That scream Nev. It was blood-curdling. I've heard the term used before, but it really was.' Tears burned her eyes as Nev put his arm around her shoulder, her half-eaten plate of food forgotten on her lap.

'You'll get them Jen. You always do.'

Nev held her as tears ran down her cheeks and dropped to her plate.

Sniffing, she lifted her head from Nev's consoling shoulder. 'Thanks. I feel okay now.' Her eyes rested on the now cold food on her plate. Her appetite was gone, but she knew she should eat.

'I'll heat it up for you.' Nev picked up the plate, put it into the microwave as Jenny reached for her beer, drinking the rest in one long, noisy gulp.

'I've not talked to Nick about your Uncle's Sorry Business.'

Last month Nev had taken her to visit his uncle in the Aboriginal Homelands. The man was an Elder and lived at the Umoona Community, when he wasn't tracking or on walk-about. He often referred to the William Creek Station curse. He also used to work for Nick's dad.

Her gut kept telling her solving Nick's mum's disappearance and answering the question of whether his dad committed suicide or not, could help solve her own missing person's case. It was clear now the William Creek Station curse and Nick's dad's death were unrelated, but she owed it to Nev and Nick to dig into it.

'That's really not your responsibility.'

'I'm the one who found his grandmother's diary.'

The microwave dinged. Nev's hand hovered over the handle, his eyes fixed on the door a moment before pulling it open.

'Have you read it?' He collected her cutlery and strolled back to the lounge, keeping his voice smooth, but his tense body told her he was curious.

'Not all of it.' She knew enough to realise Nick and Nev could be related.

'Don't keep me hanging.' He plonked down next to her.

'I'm still piecing it together and there's nothing for sure. It might not even fit the timeline. Your Uncle said he was a child when something happened in the Community. Right?'

'That's what he said.' Nev's eyes were fixed on hers.

'How old is he?' 'He's sixty-five.'

Jenny shook her head. It didn't fit the timeline. Nick's Grandmother died a few years ago, at the age of ninety.

'It's probably not the same event then.'

'What?' Nev fidgeted.

'Nick's grandma spoke about a local indigenous man she fell for. But it could be the ramblings of an old woman.'

'Uncle's story said the Johnston men rounded up six young men from the Nation and shot them, something to do with one of the Johnston women.'

'But if your uncle was a kid, say three or four, then Nick's Grandma would have been nearly thirty. That's not a young woman having an affair with a young man.'

'What did Nick's Grandma say? Did she give a name?'

Jenny put a forkful of food in her month, her appetite returning with Nev's excitement.

'You can read it for yourself if you want. I could be putting too much padding between the lines, but if I understand her correctly, she was already pregnant when those young men were shot.'

'She mentions them in the diary?' Jenny nodded. 'It has to be the same story. So Nick could be a descendent from our people?'

'You could be related! Depending on which one of those six men was her lover.'

Nev laughed aloud. 'It probably wouldn't matter which one of them fathered a Johnston kid. If he is related to any one of them, he is part of our mob.' Nev smiled. 'Nick's been good to our people. He loves Country, treats it well. It might explain a lot. Maybe he hears it calling like we do.'

'Maybe. Or maybe he knows. Maybe he read his Grandma's diary, or like your family, she told him the story.'

'The question is, do you ask him? Or do you let sleeping dogs lie?' Nev studied her a moment, then shook his head. 'It doesn't make a difference to anyone but Nick and his brother Sam. To our mob, the six men are dead and no one holds Nick or Sam responsible for that, least of all Uncle.'

'No one?' A thought hit Jenny like a bullet.

'I know that look. Don't go there.'

'Why? You think no one in the Community is capable of revenge?'

'Nick's dad was too young to have anything to do with the Sorry Business and his dad could be the baby, but our people don't hold generational grudges.'

'Maybe it's Nick's mum's story, not his gran's?' She finished off the last of her plateful, grinning mischievously.

'Now you're clutching at straws. She's definitely too young.' Nev pushed off the lounge and strolled to the fridge. Opening it, he pulled out two more beers. 'Where's that bloody diary!'

Chapter 10

The sun was bright and the air crisp but Jenny's mood was not reflecting the serenity. The rusted Dodge ute she purchased from a local miner rumbled down the main street. A loud bang signified another backfire – turning heads as she parked outside Nikolic's café.

The sight of Penny sitting at an outside table lifted her spirits. It was Penny who kept her up to date when Nick was shot and flown to Adelaide for surgery. It was Penny who accepted her late- night phone calls when there was no one else to talk to in this dusty, hot, desolate town.

'Hey. Crazy couple of days. Right!' Jenny pulled out a chair as Niko arrived with two mugs of coffee. 'Perfect timing Niko.'

'Your friend told me to get a wriggle on, but you look like you need a double shot.'

'The only double I need is a double helping of caramel syrup.' Jenny grinned.

'I can do that.' He gave her a thumbs up, and hurried back to collect the amber liquid gold to kick start her day.

'He's pretty cute.' Penny stated for at least the tenth time since she met the Serbian café owner.

'He is. Don't forget, he's a preacher's son.' Jenny knew the idea appealed to her friend. She nodded toward the counter. 'Why don't you do something about it?'

'Ha! You can talk. Have you told Nick how you feel yet?'

'He's too focussed on the station to be bothered with dating a cop and I have no idea how I feel about Nick.'

'So him coming to your rescue on your last big case and then being at the BnS Friday night is his unique way of being too tied up to notice you?' Penny lifted her eyebrows and locked eyes with Jenny.

'Oh shut up.' She slapped her friend's arm affectionately, picked up her coffee and snuck a sip before holding it up for the second shot of caramel syrup Niko was offering, bottle in hand. 'Thanks. I really do need this.' She saluted him with the cup.

'That was nasty business the other night. Marj told me all about it.' Niko said.

'Of course she did.' The local motel owner was renowned for her gossip. 'She's probably come up with at least three exaggerated scenarios by now.'

'Four.' Niko laughed and bustled back to his counter where the unmistakable suit of lawyer Samantha Hayes waited impatiently to place an order. Jenny admired the fact she found good coffee in town way faster than she had.

'Speaking of Nick. I was thinking of heading out to the station to check on him today, but I'm a bit tired from yesterday and this case is really bugging me, big time.' She leant forward over the table so no one could overhear. Especially Hayes. 'What is a swanky Melbourne lawyer doing representing band members who may be suspects in one of her senior partner's daughter's death.'

'Let's find out.' Penny waved the lawyer over.

'What are you doing?' Jenny spoke through gritting teeth. 'I can't be seen speaking with a suspect's lawyer.'

Penny ignored her entirely, making Jenny squirm and shrink low down into her chair, attempting to hide behind her coffee cup. Like that was even possible. Sarge or O'Connell would kill her if they saw them together. Her mind raced. She could say they bumped into her in the café. It was only a polite hello. Yes. That's all it was. Wasn't it?

'You're a long way from home out here.' Penny pulled out the spare chair at the table. Samantha smiled sweetly, then sat down.

'Good to see you again Penny.' Jenny looked from woman to woman and rolled her eyes skyward.

'You two know each other?'

'We've met on occasion. When was the last time?' Penny rubbed her chin as though she were genuinely trying to remember, but pursed lips said she knew exactly when it was. 'That's right. I was giving forensic evidence in that rape case you were defending.

'Now Penny. You know I don't get to choose my clients. The bosses tell me what to do.' Somehow, Jenny found that very hard to believe.

'They say jump and you jump.' Penny wasn't pulling any punches. Jenny sat back to enjoy the show.

'You don't make junior partner in a firm like Campbell, Newman and Smart without jumping. The higher the better. Come on ladies.' The lawyer was pleading her case. 'You know how hard it is in our world to reach the top jobs. You have to put all sense of femininity aside and fight like a testosterone fuelled bulldog.'

'Don't we know it.' Penny sipped her coffee as Niko arrived with Samantha's order. 'Really? Egg white omelette!'

Samantha shrugged. 'We can't all be carb queens you know.' She threw a carefully measured glare at Jenny.

'Your clients weren't held over. What's keeping you here? It can't be the lovely scenery.' Penny was asking questions Jenny wasn't sure she wanted the lawyer to answer.

'Actually. I was thinking I might do some fossicking, or what is it they call it, noodling!'

'Not in that outfit.' Penny squinted at the lawyer. 'I think you're here to keep an eye on things for Smart, considering it's your client who identified her. I find that strange.'

Jenny squirmed. They shouldn't be discussing the case with a defence attorney.

Samantha waved one finger in the air as she delicately chewed, then swallowed, sipped her coffee agonisingly slowly, then smiled angelically. 'I'd be lying if I said I didn't offer to keep Mr Smart abreast.'

'You're a lawyer Samantha, you'd be lying if you said anything.'

Chapter 11

Jenny ticked off her list of priorities for the day as she drove to work. The band footage cleared the boys from the suspect pool. They were on stage when the crowd filed out to see what happened. But now, the suspect pool was huge and they didn't know where to start.

Her first task was to call Mr and Mrs Smart. Maybe they could explain why their daughter was in Coober Pedy.

Penny was waiting on the station doorstep, waving her hand enthusiastically. Jenny crossed her fingers, hoping for some forensic lead that might point to who attacked Melinda Smart Friday night.

'You don't look very rested from yesterday.' Penny handed her a coffee from a cardboard tray.

'Even a fun-filled day of adventure with the infamous Penny McGregor can't rid me of that bloody smell. My nasal passages are still reliving Friday night.'

'I forget how it smells. It's like horse shit, you get used to it. Your nose learns to block the smell out.'

'I don't think I'll ever get used to it. Especially the burnt hair.' She stifled a gag.

Penny patted her on the arm. 'I've got some interesting info that might help you get over it. Has anyone spoken with the victim's parents yet?'

'The Melbourne police delivered the news Saturday. I half expected to see them on our doorstep yesterday or this morning.'

'They haven't flown up yet?' Penny followed Jenny inside.

'Not that I've heard. The body will go to them in Melbourne once you finish with her. Until then, they apparently asked to be kept up to date. I'll call them today.'

'They must know Samantha is here. Maybe that's enough for them?'

Jenny shrugged as she entered the quiet station foyer, opened the countertop and held it for Penny to walk through.

'I guess I'll find out soon enough.'

'Williams.' Sarge leant against his office doorframe. For once, he wasn't yelling and his toes weren't tapping impatiently on the faded lino floor.

'On my way Sarge.' Jenny tossed her backpack on O'Connell's desk, not stopping to put it in her locker.

'Close the door.' Jenny did as she was told. The sergeant's tone was calm. So why was her stomach doing summersaults?

'What's up?' She held her breath.

Sarge faced his window, arms crossed, peering out at the mines dotted over the horizon. The red and white mounds of dirt made Jenny think of a moonscape, but the drilling rigs reminded her of something out of a Mad Max movie.

'O'Connell tells me you've been sniffing around Nick's dad's suicide case?'

O'Connell never promised to keep quiet about her enquiries into Nick's family history. He only promised he wouldn't tell Sergeant Mackenzie she took the job in Coober Pedy to find out about to her cousin and aunt.

She was speechless. Getting sent back to Adelaide wasn't an option. Her investigation into Melanie and Aunt Carolyn's disappearance had barely started.

'I have. Is that a problem Sir?' She forced herself to keep calm.

'Have you found anything out of place?' The question was casual, but so unexpected that Jenny was too surprised to answer at first.

'An autopsy wasn't conducted. Penny believes it probably should have been, especially considering Nick's mum Patricia disappeared at the same time.'

Sergeant Mackenzie sighed, then shook his head. 'I hope we didn't miss anything.'

A chill run down her spine. His voice was so quiet. 'I'm sure it will be fine Sir. I want to help Nick put some pieces together. If I can give him some closure, at least he'll be satisfied we did our job properly.'

Sergeant Mackenzie was in a drunken stupor over his daughter's death when Nick's dad died, around the same time Melanie and Aunt Carolyn went missing, so if anyone dropped the ball, it was going to be Len Holmes. Of course, Len was only covering for Sarge and any anomalies in the cases, if found, would come back to her boss, not Len.

She thought about what Kent Murphy said when Nick was shot. 'Mr Murphy.' The Sergeant turned to face her still standing by his desk.

'What about him?' He frowned, swivelled his office chair around and sat.

'He said something, when Nick got shot.' She saw the scene play out again in her mind and suppressed a shudder. 'He said Nick was tough like his mum. How well did he know Patricia Johnston?'

'You heard rumours then.' It wasn't a question.

'Some.'

'If you think Murphy killed old man Johnston to get Patricia in his bed, you're barking up the wrong tree Williams.' The usual gruff tone was back.

'I honestly don't care if they were sleeping together Sir. Nick might, but I don't. What I'm wondering though, is did Patricia Johnston confide in him? Did he know if Nick's dad was suffering from depression? Did he know she was going to

54

disappear and why? For all we know, Patricia Johnston could be dead. Len never bothered to follow up.'

'I see where you're going.' Jenny knew Murphy and her boss were close. 'I'll chat with Kent. See what I can garner.'

'Nick and Sam need to put their past behind them. I'm hoping we can help.' *And find out what happened to my family.*

'Let's get this briefing done. Where are we at with this case?' Sarge rose, circled around his desk and headed to the office door. He held it for her to go through, then joined her in the main office. 'Let's get this unpacked people.'

'Philips. Where are we at with all the witness videos?' Philips turned from the front counter, his body drawing up to attention.

'I've downloaded it all Sir. Williams and I will be running through it today.' The phone rang, O'Connell lifted his desk phone handset.

'Williams, keep me informed once you speak with Smart. I don't like that his junior partner was here representing the band. She got here awfully quick.'

'Will do Sir. We ran the band members for priors, nothing popped up. The video they provided cleared them all. They were on stage when I witnessed Melinda's attack.'

Jenny was distracted by O'Connell's call. Her eyes flicked between Sarge and him.

'McGregor. What you got so far?'

'Good news really. The toxicology came back first thing this morning. There were no drugs or foreign substances in the victim's system. Her alcohol reading was under .012, and the accelerant used was diesel, as we suspected.'

'So that's the good news?' Sarge pursed his lips.

'No. The good news is although her blood work was clean, we did find traces of Methamphetamine on her clothing.'

'Drugs. It's always bloody drugs with you young people.'

No one responded. Jenny and Penny exchanged a look. It was always funny how the baby boomers were the ones to point the finger at recreational drug users.

The acid, heroin and marijuana of the sixties was way heavier than a few ecstasy pills at a BnS or rave but she wasn't about to ruin her new working relationship with her boss by pointing it out. Yesterday maybe, but not today.

'Let's not start the drug debate Sir. You're talking to a scientist. The popular cods-wallop handed out by the media and government isn't exactly scientifically supported.' Penny's mounting tirade was interrupted by O'Connell as he hung up.

'That was Marj. She's found the purse we've been searching for. The one Williams saw under the truck Friday night.'

'Empty, I'm guessing.' Jenny lifted her backpack from O'Connell's desk and rushed to her locker. 'I'll head over with Penny to grab it.'

'Marj hasn't touched it. She's set up a perimeter, with tinsel,' O'Connell sniggered. 'Would you believe it.'

'Totally plausible. Gotta love that woman. Too many TV murder mysteries up her sleeve.'

'Let's go.' Penny grabbed her forensic kit from under the counter. 'We'll continue this conversation over beers tonight Sir.' She goaded Jenny's Boss. 'It's an interesting debate. Legalising recreational drugs to free up law enforcement so they can deal with other serious crime.'

'Don't get him started.' O'Connell waggled his finger in warning. 'Feeding more money into pharmaceutical companies. The last thing we need.'

Jenny grinned at Penny as they hurried from the station, bursting into giggles as soon as they left the building. Crossing the road, they followed the red, dusty sidewalk around to the front of the motel.

'I can grab this alone if you have other work to get on with.'

'It's okay. I want to ask Marj a few questions and show her a photo of Melinda.'

'Okay. Sounds good.'

They crossed the bright green artificial lawn in front of the motel reception area. It was a vivid contrast to the dry, dirty carpark and roadside. A few planted gumtrees and shrubs were all that broke up the red, white and sulphur covered desert surrounding Coober Pedy.

Penny followed the concrete path around the side where they could see red and silver tinsel fluttering in the light breeze, while Jenny ducked her head into the office. 'Marj.' The office was empty. Jenny frowned, wondering where the ever-present motel owner was.

'Out here!'

She stepped through to the carpark side of the office, joining Penny by the commercial bins.

'Great job Marj. You can leave it with Penny now.' The big busted redhead grinned triumphantly.

'I've not let anyone near the place since I found it.' She scanned over her shoulder like a spy. 'I heard you were looking for a purple purse and I found it when I came out to empty the bins.'

Jenny wondered how Marj knew about the purse. No public statement was issued yet. No one even canvassed businesses about Melinda yet. The woman was an anomaly.

'I don't suppose you have cameras out here?' Marj shook her head. Jenny pulled her phone out of her pocket and brought up a photo of Melinda Smart. 'Have you seen this woman in town?'

She studied the photo carefully, then shook her head again. 'That BnS was held out at Sullivan's property, in the old hangar. Most of those kids were from outlying stations or camping out there for the weekend.'

'Some probably came in to town for supplies and maybe some grabbed a beer at the bar?'

Marj shrugged. 'Ask Stan or Cheryl. They've been on shift most of the weekend. Or the new girl, Kelly. Then you should try Jeremy's store, or better still, the bottle-shop in town. They likely all bought cartons of beer or those lolly water cruiser thingies for the weekend.'

'Thanks Marj.' Maybe watching TV murder mysteries wasn't entirely a waste of time. 'I'll do that.'

Melinda's alcohol levels were low, so the bottle-shop wasn't high on Jenny's list, but everyone needed to eat. Jeremy's market made the top of her to-do list for the day. She knew she was putting off calling Mr and Mrs Smart, but what kind of parent sends a junior lawyer to oversee a case where their daughter was brutally attacked?

'You're right. It's empty.' Penny lifted the purse. 'But there's traces of something on the silky interior. Let me take a swab.' She drew a test kit out of her bag, opened it and wiped the test strip over the inside of the bag, touching the sides and bottom of the purse. She then slipped the strip into a solution, shook it gently and waited.

A colour began to appear almost immediately, but Penny set a timer on her watch and waited. 'Give it a few more seconds, but I think this is another positive for MDMA.'

'So three positive tests for MDMA. The truck, the purse and Melinda's clothing. But we can't link the purse to the victim yet. Except I believe Jake knows whoever it was that owned the purple purse.'

'Why do you say that?'

'Call it gut instinct, but his face went pale when I asked about a girl with the purple bag. He wasn't going to say he knew her until Hayes made him own up.'

'Maybe you should take another look at the band.'

Jenny shook her head. 'I don't see how they are involved in Melinda's murder. They were all on stage at the time. But they know something they're not telling me.'

Chapter 12

Penny came out of Sergeant Mackenzie's office, stopped and glanced over her shoulder. 'You probably have twenty-four hours before my test results set off alarm bells. Then maybe twelve before a detective is assigned.'

'We'll play this one by the book.' Sergeant Mackenzie gazed up as Penny took the clutch bag to the breakroom she converted into her lab. 'O'Connell, get on to the task force in Adelaide. We'll be on the front foot for this one.'

'Yes Sir.' O'Connell looked ready to say more, but lifted the handset to make the call.

Jenny wondered if her earlier conversation about Nick's dad's death was influencing Sarge's cooperative attitude.

'Coober Pedy isn't exactly a huge drug market. I have a feeling they'll be slow on the uptake in any case, but we don't want to be seen dragging our feet.' Sarge appeared calm.

'We can hope so.' O'Connell dialled and waited.

'Let's go over what we have.' Sergeant Mackenzie sat on the corner of O'Connell's desk as Penny returned to the main office. 'Anything in the interviews Saturday jump out at you?' Sarge glanced at Jenny for an answer.

'So far, we still don't have a motive for killing Melinda Smart, but the band are being represented by her father's firm. At first, Jake claimed he didn't know the victim, but it was Hayes who insisted he tell me. Jake quickly dropped off the suspect list though when Curtis produced a video showing all the band on stage at the time of the murder.'

'And the Meth? You said you got a hit on the truck, the purse and our victim's clothing.' Sergeant Mackenzie turned to Penny.

'On her clothing, yes, but she wasn't using. Her toxicology screening was all clear.'

'One pill doesn't make this a major drug crime.' He rubbed his chin and tapped his lip with his index finger.

O'Connell hung up. 'The detectives on the drug initiative team seem to agree with you Sir.'

'They aren't coming?' His eyebrows rose.

'Not yet. Link the girl's death to drug dealers or bikie activity and they'll be on the next flight. I'm quoting Detective Anderson Sir.'

'So we are clear to proceed team.' Sarge shared a rare smile.

'And they aren't handing the death over to homicide?' Jenny frowned.

'They said our clearance rate was good enough not to warrant it unless it escalates to more than one victim.' O'Connell's grin grew wider.

'Let's get on with it then. My head is spinning.' Sarge rubbed his temples.

Philips lifted the countertop and stumbled into the office, his feet covered in red dirt, his uniform showed dark sweat stains down the middle of his back and under his arms.

'Hell, it's hot today. I've been to every bottle shop, pub, and accommodation booking agency in town and Williams already checked the grocery store. No one has seen Melinda Smart or taken a booking under her name.'

'So we are back to square one. Let's check incoming flights, car rentals. Someone must have seen this young woman.' O'Connell clapped his hands like a school teacher bringing an unruly class to attention.

Jenny turned toward the front counter as a woman in her early twenties, wearing olive-coloured shorts and an off-the-shoulder blouse wandered into the station. Her doe-like eyes studied them from under a straw cowgirl hat.'

The words out of her mouth made Jenny's heart skip a beat.

'I'd like to report a missing person.'

Chapter 13

Philips handed the petite woman a box of tissues as Jenny put a cup of white tea on the table in front of her.

'When did you last see Melinda?' Jenny led the interview.

'Around eleven o'clock at the BnS. I shouldn't have left her alone.' She sniffed and wiped her nose.

'It's not your fault Rachel. You didn't know this was going to happen.'

'But I should have...' Jenny frowned as the young woman visibly forced her mouth shut. Did she know something she wasn't sharing? Or was it just guilt?

Jenny fidgeted with the pen in her hand. There was a reason she preferred to take notes on her phone. Pen and paper nearly always resulted in her biting the pen or doodling on the paper.

'Do you know anyone who might have wanted to hurt Melinda?'

'No!' The answer was too quick. Too defensive. Rachel's hand shook as she put her fingers on the teacup.

'Did you see Melinda fighting with anyone Friday night?' An uncomfortable silence grew. Rachel filled the gap by lifting the tea to her lips and sipping slowly. 'Rachel. Someone tossed diesel on your friend and set her alight!'

Jenny's patience was waning. Rachel knew more than she was saying. Absolutely everyone poured from the shed Friday night. Once one person heard Melinda's screams and saw Nick roll her in the dirt to put the fire out, the word travelled fast. Why wasn't Rachel in the crowd?

'I know! But I can't help you.' She wiped her nose again.

Jenny made a show of writing down the answer, then peering intently into Rachel's eyes searching for answers. The woman squirmed under the scrutiny.

'Where were you when Melinda was killed? Why has it taken you nearly three days to report her missing?' Jenny thought about the purse, with the MDMA trace evidence. Penny found fingerprints, but there was no suspect to compare them to.

'I passed out.' Her shoulders dropped. Her eyes fell to her lap, focussing on her wringing hands.

'Were you with anyone?'

'No.' The word was barely whispered. Jenny's gut rolled. Rachel was holding something back, but pushing wasn't going to get her the answers she needed.

'How did you know Melinda?' The question was the right one. Rachel's face softened, but she kept her eyes downcast, her hands still fidgeting.

'We went to school together.'

She must know Jake then. Jenny kept the thought to herself. There was no way of knowing if mentioning the singer was a good idea. She needed Rachel talking, and relaxed.

'Which school was that?' She kept her tone neutral. It was working. Rachel made eye-contact and held it.

'St Louis Grammar.'

'Nice school?'

Rachel shrugged. 'It's prestigious.'

'And you came here, to Coober Pedy for the BnS, together?'

'Yes. Road tripped up here in her dad's Mercedes G-Wagon.'

Of course you did. Probably complete with bulletproof glass. 'I'm going to ask you again where you've been for the past two and half days Rachel. I understand you might have been out cold when Melinda died, but why not report her missing when you woke up Saturday? Surely you heard gossip about a girl being set on fire the night before?'

There was a moment of uncomfortable silence. Rachel's expressions twisted, her eyes flicked from Jenny to Philips and back again.

'I was scared.' Her voice quivered. There it was. The truth at last.

'Of who?' Tears welled in her eyes. She reached for another tissue, saying nothing, her eyes not meeting Jenny's.

She made a show of blowing her nose, then peering around the room, now avoiding eye-contact at any cost. Her brow creased, her lips thinned. Jenny needed to calm her down quickly or she would bolt out the door. There was no reason to hold her.

'We can protect you Rachel.' Jenny patted the back of her hand reassuringly.

She snatched it away. 'I don't need protecting. I don't know anything.' Her eyes were back on her hands, in her lap.

'Do you want me to call your parents? Boyfriend?'

'Call Nigel Smart. I need to talk with him.'

Why was Rachel asking for a lawyer?

'I'm going to need to take your fingerprints Rachel, for elimination. I'd also like to know where Melinda's car is. We need to search it.' Standing, she turned to leave the interview just as the door opened, nearly hitting her in the face.

'Constable Williams. Thank you for looking after my client.' The tone was forced sweet. The smile matching.

Standing in the doorway as immaculately groomed as always was Samantha Hayes.

'Your client?' Jenny glanced over her shoulder. Rachel's eyes went wide. She pushed back into her seat, visibly distancing herself from Hayes. 'Rachel was simply reporting a missing person.' Jenny returned her gaze to Hayes.

'How did you know Rachel was here?' Philips half rose, as Hayes sashayed around the table to stand alongside Rachel's chair.

'That's confidential Constable.' She pulled Rachel to her feet with enough force to elicit a grimace. 'Let's go. Your dad's expecting you on the next flight home.'

'That won't be possible.' Jenny blocked their exit. Her arms crossed. Her legs splayed.

'And why not Constable.'

Jenny let her eyebrows rise in question. How does a woman go from pleasant to full-on panther at lightning speed?

'Because she is a material witness in an ongoing murder investigation.'

'Melinda Smart's death isn't homicide. It's death by misadventure if I'm not mistaken. I don't see a detective anywhere.' Hayes made a show of searching over her shoulder, and under the table. She thought she was being funny.

Jenny smiled, not bothering to cover her smugness. She loved a good fight as much as the next person. 'A report was filed with Major Crimes. They've left the murder investigation with us unless it escalates. You can check with Detective Anderson in Adelaide if you want to confirm. I didn't speak with him, Senior Constable O'Connell did, but he's with the Major Crimes Task Force.'

'I'll keep Rachel in town.' Hayes tugged the woman out of the interview room. Rachel pulled away from the lawyer's grip.

Jenny wanted to rip the lawyer's arm off Rachel's, but resisted the urge. 'We need prints and access to Melinda's car before Rachel goes anywhere. You can leave her with me. I'll make sure she gets home safely.' Rachel's eyes darted from

Jenny, to Hayes. Her expression muddled, her body rigid. It was clear she didn't want to go anywhere with Hayes.

Hayes studied Jenny's face a moment, then forced another congenial smile. 'You win this round Constable.'

Damn right I do!

Chapter 14

Jenny collected the jug of beer from the bar, along with a tower of chilled glasses, precariously balanced. Penny followed right behind her with a glass of wine and a fistful of various flavoured potato chips. They wove their way through the dining room toward a long table, centrally located between the bar and the function room at the back of the restaurant.

Penny slid into a chair alongside Philips. 'So what did Smart have to say?'

O'Connell and Sergeant Mackenzie shuffled glasses around the table as Jenny poured beer. 'He wouldn't take my calls. Neither would his wife.' Jenny peered at the empty beer jug, then pushed it to the middle of the table – code for next round was someone else's.

'That sets off warning bells right there. I'd have been here, not fending off calls from the police if it were my daughter.' Sarge sculled half his beer in one mouthful.

If anyone knew what losing a child was like it was her boss. It lightened Jenny's spirit to see him join in for a beer though. Maybe Penny's challenge revved him up?

'So that begs the question. Is Smart complicit in something which caused his daughter's death or afraid of something? Or is her murder totally unrelated to whatever he's trying to hide?' Jenny popped the top of a packet of plain potato chips.

'We need to do some more digging into Smart's clients, associates. That's your job tomorrow Williams.' Sarge sculled his beer. 'Round two is on me.'

****

Jenny stuck a small, pink adhesive note to the new standing mirror she picked up from the Op Shop. Tim made a few jokes about her not being the vain type when he helped her carry the over-sized mirror in and settle it against the wall at the end of her bed.

At the time, she laughed along, not wanting to explain what the mirror was for. A piece of rolled sticky tape held the photos of Melanie and Aunt Carolyn in place, front and centre of her mirror crime board.

Drinks at the motel were fun. Spending social time with her boss proved more relaxing than she expected. She grinned recalling Penny and Sarge going head-to-head over the legalising of drugs.

They all had early starts in the morning, but Jenny came home wired. Sleep wasn't coming any time soon, so she sat on her bed, staring at the makeshift map of her investigation into her missing relatives.

She now knew Melanie and Aunt Carolyn stayed at the William Creek Pub and according to Mrs B., the pub owner, skipped out on their bill. That wasn't in their character and the more she thought about it, the more she realised they were either taken or left in an urgent fluster.

Since there was ample proof Melanie was seen with Nick's dad at William Creek Station after they left the pub, foul play was unlikely, unless Nick's dad was a deviate – and she refused to go there at this stage.

Melanie's handwriting was found in the accounts ledger. So she was willingly doing the books for Nick's mum, which made it far more likely Melanie was working at the station. But why? She and Aunt Carolyn were on a short holiday before Mel went to Uni. Maybe Aunt Carolyn left her there to work, to get used to the idea of working her way through university?

Jenny shrugged. That didn't make sense. If that's what happened, where was Aunt Carolyn during Mel's stint at the station, and where the hell were they now?

No matter which way she looked at it, Nick's dad's death and his mother's disappearance were her only link to what might have happened to her aunt and cousin. She pulled out the file she downloaded of Nick's dad's suicide and placed two photos of the scene on her mirror board. The photo of Nick's dad, slumped on the kitchen table made her shiver. She studied it closely, biting her lip. The rifle was in Mr Johnston's right hand, lying flat on the table. Would a gun be resting neatly under his hand if he shot himself with it?

Sighing, she turned away from the gruesome photos, her mind drifting to Nick and his crystal blue eyes. She wished she'd kept her promise and visited him on Sunday. Would he be mad with her?

Checking the time, she picked up her mobile. Eleven was too late to call. He'd see a text in the morning. She began typing.

It's late, so I'm texting so you get this in the morning. Hope the hand is okay. Playing hero seems to be biting you in the butt. But it's appreciated. Just wanted to check on you. Sorry I didn't make it to yours on Sunday. Did Rebecca have any new ideas about the ledger? Thanks Jenny.

Her finger hovered over the X button, but she hit send instead, then tossed the phone on her bed.

It buzzed almost as soon as it landed. Looking down, she saw it was ringing. Nick was still awake.

Sliding the bar over, she answered. 'I didn't mean to wake you.'

'You didn't.'

What was he doing up, all alone at night? Maybe he wasn't alone. Maybe, like her, he couldn't sleep?

'Rebecca didn't know what the notations in the ledger were, sorry, I know how important this is to you.'

She wondered what might have happened between Nick and the station administrator Rebecca if his dad were still alive. Everyone expected them to get married. Would they have kids by now? Her gut told her unlikely.

'Did you read that old diary in the end?' He didn't wait for her to answer. 'Maybe you can come out this weekend and we can search the cellar for more clues.'

She smiled at how he said clues, then wondered if she should mention the diary contents? It wasn't relevant to either of their family cases, but Nick should probably know, if he didn't already.

'I read the diary. Have you?' She held her breath.

'I didn't even know it was there.'

'It doesn't matter. We don't need an excuse to catch up, do we? I should be available Sunday.'

'Great. I'll be in touch.' Then he was gone. Jenny stared at the phone screen, bewildered.

Did he just ask me out for a date? She put the phone on her bedside. Don't read too much into it. You're here to solve a family mystery. Don't get side-tracked!

She returned her attention to getting ready for bed, but as she considered her oversized mirror, she didn't see the photos and sticky notes all over it. She saw the stupid, schoolgirl grin on her face and swiftly wiped it away.

Chapter 15

'Rachel.' Jenny sat with Philips across the table from the petite woman. 'We found your fingerprints at the scene of Melinda's murder.'

'Constable. Rachel has already admitted to being at the scene. She's admitted to having a relationship with two of the band members.' The lawyer's expression was smug. Jenny wondered how the lawyer knew they were bringing Rachel in for questioning again. Rachel certainly didn't look like she called her in.

'Yes. We know, but we also found footprints appearing to belong to a female on the scene.' Her voice cracked. She cleared her throat. The smell of smoke lingered in her nostrils. 'And a purple purse was stolen from our scene. Rachel's fingerprints were found on the purse along with traces of MDMA.'

'You say you saw it at the scene. There are no crime scene photos to support that this purse,' Hayes pointed to a forensic photo of the bag, taken in Penny's makeshift lab, 'is the same purse you saw on scene.'

She was right. She was totally and absolutely right. Jenny seethed on the inside, but a light, cheerful smile crossed her lips.

'Of course. That is true, but either way, the purse has traces of MDMA on it and your client's fingerprints. We'll be holding her over in our cells while we continue our investigation in relation to drug charges, and the possible production of methamphetamine.'

Jenny knew it was a long stretch to go from traces of MDMA in the purse to production and dealing of meth, but it was an offence warranting detainment and Jenny wanted to keep Hayes away from Rachel.

Hayes's smug smile dissipated. 'Don't even think about questioning my client without me present.'

'You're going to have your hands full then. Jake is likely to face the same charges.'

'You've got nothing on him. I heard your evidence blew up.' The smug expression was back. Jenny studied Hayes as she sat back into her chair, her arms crossed over her chest.

'And you wouldn't know anything about that, now would you?'

'I don't know what you're implying Constable, but you are way out of line and so far out of your depth. Tread lightly.'

Was that a threat? Someone was happy to let her burn in that shed. She peered under the table a moment. Hayes uncrossed her legs self-consciously, then pushed back her chair and rose.

'Rachel. I'll have you out on bail in no time. They've got nothing substantial on you. Stay put, shut up and it will all be fine. You can go home to mummy and daddy, free and safe.'

Tears sprang to Rachel's eyes as the lawyer strutted to the door.

'Oh. Ms Hayes,' Jenny used her sweetest voice. The woman turned, scowling with extra effort. 'can you please track down Curtis Greenfield? He is required for further questioning and we didn't confirm his contact information, so he isn't clear to leave town.'

The lawyer hesitated, returned her eyes to the half-open door and left without another word. As the door slammed closed, Jenny turned to see Rachel bury her head in her hands and begin to sob.

'Rachel.' She shook her head without lifting it. 'Rachel, listen to me. I can see you don't want Hayes representing you. I tried Nigel Smart, but he isn't taking any calls.' Rachel said nothing, but her eyes were fixed on Jenny's. 'You need to talk to me. Let's start with where you left the Mercedes.'

****

Jenny scribbled on the whiteboard set up in the Sergeant's office, away from prying eyes.

'What are you thinking Williams?' O'Connell sat on the corner of the desk, Sarge leant back in his seat, while Philips waited by the door, one eye on the front desk.

'You guys dug up information on Smart. He's connected, right? Harlequin gang kind of connected.'

'Not necessarily him, but his firm certainly is. It's Hayes who has represented the Harlequins in a dozen cases. From drugs to prostitution and even one count of torture by the former President of the gang.'

Jenny made more notes on the whiteboard, adding Hayes's name with an arrow from Melinda's autopsy photo. 'That makes sense to me. We have a female footprint on the scene which is too large for Rachel. Whoever the footprint belongs to, took the purse from the scene and later dumped it. They could be our murderer. Hayes could be that person.'

'I get why you don't like her, but Hayes didn't arrive until the band members came in for questioning.' O'Connell joined the theorising.

'She got here pretty early the next morning. Have we checked to see if she was on the first flight in?' Jenny added date of arrival to Hayes' name on the board.

'I'll run that now.' Philips ducked out of the office excitedly.

'We are assuming Smart fast-tracked Hayes to junior partner in record time. I've still not been able to get Smart on the phone. His daughter has been brutally murdered, and he won't take my calls.' Jenny wrote SMART and joined his name with another line to his dead daughter's photo.

74

Jenny studied the photo of the burnt woman's body. The shrill scream sounded in the recesses of her mind. She shuddered, then forced herself to focus on the whiteboard.

'You sure you should be back on duty?' Sergeant Mackenzie half rose, as though he expected her to faint. His recent change of attitude was most welcome, most of the time, but she didn't do damsel in distress. She waved her hand before he got to his feet.

'I'm fine Sir.'

'We have to ask the question if the victim was innocent in all this or a part of it?' O'Connell made a solid point.

'Her bank records show she gets an allowance from her father.' Philips returned to the room. 'The earliest flight in on Sunday morning was ten a.m..'

'Was Hayes on it?' Jenny held the whiteboard marker, poised to take notes.

'I'm waiting for the manifest, but she was here by ten thirty. Even with carry-on luggage only, that's a close timeline.'

'Doable, but yeah, very close.' Jenny conceded.

Sergeant Mackenzie's eyes found Philips. 'Keep on the airline. We need that manifest.' He pointed his finger.

'Will do Sarge.'

'Okay, so Melinda is a trust fund child. No career then?' Philips shook his head. 'No record of large deposits?' Another shake. 'Can we check Rachel's bank accounts?' Jenny asked O'Connell the question.

'Not without a warrant.'

'We have to lay formal charges to get that and we don't have enough evidence.' Sarge said.

'I don't think Rachel did anything wrong. I can't see her killing her best friend.' Jenny sighed.

'Penny found MDMA on the truck and Curtis has disappeared. Maybe he's the connection?' Philips offered.

'Has anyone managed to get a hold of his sister? He said she was expecting a baby.' Jenny scanned the faces. It was on her list to do yesterday but finding the purse at the motel put her behind schedule.

'Not yet. O'Connell pointed to Jenny. 'You can call her today. If he's not there, she might know where he could be.'

'Will do.'

'I trust we have McGregor going over the Mercedes' contents?' Sarge sat in his office chair, his hands laced behind the back of his head.

'Yes Sir.'

'I want a report as soon as she is done.' He waved them out, indicating the briefing was over.

Jenny pulled the door closed behind her. Philips leant in closely. 'You really think Hayes took the purse from the BnS the other night?'

'The footprints aren't Rachel's, or the victim's, so who else's could it be?'

'If she was on the flight, she couldn't have been at the BnS.' Philips stepped up to the counter computer, clicked the email open and waited.

Jenny shrugged. 'Exactly. If she was on the flight. If she wasn't, we need to keep digging.

We still don't have any motive for why anyone wanted Melinda Smart dead.'

'True.' Philips scrolled through his email. 'Hey!'

'What?' Jenny stepped up to peer over his shoulder.

'She was on the flight, according to the manifest anyway.'

'Damn it.'

'Looks like you're back to the whiteboard.' O'Connell's eyes glinted with amusement over his reading glasses. 'We'll get there Williams. Your instincts are good. If your gut thinks something isn't quite right with Hayes, just keep digging.'

'Will do Sir.' Her voice croaked, she coughed, tears sprang to her eyes, she coughed some more. Philips appeared with a glass of water. 'Thanks,' her voice rasped.

'Take a break. Grab an early lunch Williams.' O'Connell made it clear it wasn't a suggestion. She saluted with a smile.

Chapter 16

Jenny needed food. Lots of it. Her brain was foggy and a good dose of carbs would kick it back into gear. Crossing the road, she ducked her head into Motel Reception on the way to the restaurant.

'Morning Marj.' The woman was always smiling and ready to brighten everyone's day and Jenny needed a dose of happy, today more than usual.

'Good morning to you too.' Marj scurried around the counter, a twinkle in her eye that Jenny was only too familiar with. She had gossip, or wanted gossip. 'What's going on – have you caught the person who set that poor girl on fire? Everyone in town is on edge you know.'

'On edge you reckon?' Jenny grinned. 'There's no reason to believe this was some sort of rampage Marj.'

'Well how do you explain your own flaunt with fire then?' Her finger waggled in Jenny's face.

How does she find out about this stuff so fast?

'Wrong place, wrong time.' Jenny wasn't about to explain the incident to Marj. As much as she valued the woman as a friend, Marj's imagination was vivid and this was an ongoing investigation.

'So you haven't caught the mongrel yet?' Marj's brow creased with genuine concern.

'We're working on it.' Something caught her eye. Turning, she gazed across the artificial grass to see Samantha Hayes scurrying from room seven toward a fancy black sports car. The lawyer jumped into the passenger's side. Jenny stared, focussed on the scene, her heart picking up pace as curiosity piqued.

Marj saw where Jenny was focussed. 'She's a piece of work that one.' The motel owner didn't hide a sneer.

'What do you mean?' Jenny eye's remained fixed on the metallic black door as it slammed closed. The car tyres spun, kicking gravel into the air as the vehicle turned around the carpark and pulled out onto the main road. Jenny's skin tingled and it wasn't from the deep, throaty sound of the V8 engine roaring away. She desperately needed to know who was driving that car.

'Comes in all la de da, makeup, heels, throws her weight around like she's the Queen and I'm her bloody personal butler. Then, just when you think she's from the top part of town, some thug, with tattoos from arm-to-arm books in to her room.' Marj was all theatrics, her hand splaying over her shoulders and arms, her lips pursed, her chest all puffed out like a prize fighter.

Jenny supressed a grin, but her mind spun like a roulette wheel. Tattoos, lots of tattoos. 'No accounting for taste I guess.' Jenny turned to leave. 'I've got to grab a quick lunch.'

'You take your time luv. You've been in the wars. Nearly burned alive and all that, you sure you're not dealing with a serial arsonist or something?'

'No Marj, this is murder. Plain and simple.' Jenny waved before rushing toward the restaurant, her stomach grumbling. Her mind raced as she opened the double glass doors. Did she lie to Marj? There was nothing simple about this case.

Samantha's boyfriend having tatts wasn't unusual. Tattoos were common, more common than body-piercing in popularity for the twenty to thirty-year-old age group of middle-class Australians with money to burn.

But Marj described the guy as a thug. Her gut tossed and rolled. MDMA on the truck, in the purse and now a rough nut with tatts shacking up with the Harlequin connected lawyer. Was she joining dots that weren't there?

'You were quick?' O'Connell peered over his reading glasses as Jenny opened the countertop and rushed into the office area.

'I'm a fast eater.' She raced to the main desktop computer, clicked a few buttons and opened the file she needed.

Her mind ran at a million miles an hour and not even a huge bowl of chicken pesto pasta, which usually released enough endorphins to settle her anxiety, stilled her brain. Her subconscious screamed at her to remember something, something important.

'What's on your mind?' O'Connell remained seated. His eyes followed her anxious movements.

'Where's Philips?' Jenny gazed around. Sarge's door was open. His desk was empty. 'And Sarge?'

'Philips is looking for Curtis. No one has seen him.'

'I need to try his sister in Brisbane.'

'We tried while you were at lunch. She's unreachable so far.' O'Connell watched her closely. Standing, he approached the counter behind her.

Jenny searched and found the file Curtis gave them of the band playing when Melinda was killed. She rewound it, played it, then rewound it further, hoping she could find what was niggling at her. 'I'll try calling again in a minute. I just need to…'

She rewound it another thirty seconds and studied the footage closely. 'Damn. How did I miss that?'

'What? We've all watched that video a dozen times.' O'Connell peered over her shoulder, watching the footage as she did, his eyes squinting.

'Look.' Jenny rewound it again as O'Connell drew closer, adjusted his reading glasses as she hit play. 'See that?'

'No.' He frowned. 'All four members are in camera, they stay on stage until the crowd head out to see what the commotion is about.'

She rewound it one more time and played it back in slow motion. 'See him.'

'The guy with the tattoos?'

'Yes Sir. Marj just told me that Hayes has a roommate at the motel, with lots of tattoos.'

'And you think this is the same guy?'

'I think there is a good chance it is and he was nowhere in sight when we conducted interviews Friday night.' Her stomach was doing summersaults. 'I'll try Curtis's sister again. I also want to run a number plate. If Curtis doesn't turn up, will we have grounds to check his phone records?'

O'Connell rubbed his chin as he rewound the video and pressed play. 'Damn you are good.' He smiled, bringing his attention back to her question. 'Yes, if we believe he has vital information in this case, or he's a possible victim, we can likely get a warrant for his phone records. The only issue is, we do have to tell his lawyer.'

'She'll definitely kick up a stink.' Jenny lifted the office phone and dialled the number on file for Bethany Clark, Curtis's sister. 'Maybe she's gone into labour?' Jenny waited a few more rings, until the answering machine kicked in.

'Ms Clark. This is Constable Williams from the Coober Pedy Police Station. If you could call me back when you get this message, I'd appreciate it.' She read off the station number and her mobile before hanging up. Moving back to the computer, she began running the number plate for the black sports car. 'I also saw Hayes get into a car at the motel. I'm running the plate now.'

'You do that. I'll call Philips and see where he's at with finding Curtis.'

Jenny logged on to the registration office database, typed in the number plate and waited. 'I have an idea how we might be able to get Rachel talking.'

'We can't question her without her lawyer present.' O'Connell's brow creased, his posture stiffened.

'We can if she denies counsel. I won't ask her a question, I promise.' Jenny crossed her heart with her finger.

'You've got a hunch.' O'Connell squinted as he watched her.

'I do. When Hayes was with her, Rachel was on edge. She wanted me to get Nigel Smart on the phone, but he isn't taking calls. If I'm right, I think she might forgo her lawyer.'

'Oh, now that would piss off Miss Fancy Pants for sure.' O'Connell's grin told her he liked the Melbourne snobby nosed lawyer about as much as she did.

'Sir!' The registration details flicked up on the screen and the vehicle owner wasn't who she was expecting.

Chapter 17

Jenny's brain hurt. The black Audi was registered to Campbell, Newman and Smart, but the lawyer was supposed to have flown up, not driven up. They were missing something and Rachel held the key, she was sure of it.

The only problem was, they had to charge her or release her today and Jenny didn't want to charge her.

She watched the woman lying curled up on the stretcher bed in the small, brightly lit cell as she approached. Rachel's prints were on the purple clutch, complete with traces of MDMA, but in Jenny's mind, it wasn't a motive for murder.

'Rachel.' The woman didn't stir. 'I've brought you a cup of tea.'

'My lawyer said not to talk to you.' Her back was to Jenny and her face was hidden below a lightweight blanket.

'It's just a cup of tea. Besides, I didn't think you liked your lawyer very much.' The woman rolled over, her eyes scanning Jenny from head to toe. They were red-rimmed with mascara and eyeliner streaks down her face.

She tossed the thin blanket to the floor before sitting.

Good sign. 'Here. I'll open the door.' Jenny put the tea down on the side bench and pressed a pin pad to open the Perspex holding cell. She locked it open and picked up the tea before entering.

'I just want to go home.' She looked young. So naïve. So vulnerable.

'I understand. Coober Pedy is an acquired taste.' The joke didn't elicit the laugh she was hoping for but the eye roll would do for now. She leant down and handed the tea to Rachel.

'Curtis said he was heading back to visit his sister before the baby arrived.' Jenny pulled up a plastic chair, trying to create a comfortable atmosphere.

'I wouldn't know.'

'Oh. Sorry. When Ms Hayes mentioned your relationship with two of the band members, I assumed Curtis was one of them.' Another eye roll. It was better than being told to get lost.

'It's tricky though. I've not been able to get a hold of his sister either. Curtis hasn't flown out to Brisbane on any local planes or travelled on a bus.'

Rachel's cup of tea hovered in front of her lips.

'I went to call his mum or dad, but they're deceased. That must be hard for Curtis. Just him and his sister alone.'

'Why are you telling me this?' The cup of tea forgotten.

'Oh. Just chatting. Sorry. I'll leave you to finish your tea.' Jenny stood, put the chair back where it came from and stepped toward the door. She drew on her school drama classes to pull off a nervous pause, her hand hovering on the latch, ready to turn.

She creased her brow, trying for a worried expression, then turned to face Rachel. 'I'm concerned he might be missing. If he knows anything about Melinda's murder, he could be in danger.'

Jenny turned back to pull the door shut, hoping Rachel would bite.

'Ms Williams.' The sound of Samantha Hayes' over enunciated words made her jump. 'I told you not to interview my client without me being present. Didn't I?' The lawyer's hands flew to her hips, a sneer on her lips.

'I think the title you are searching for is Constable Williams.' Jenny locked the door, then strutted to step in front of the lawyer.

'You were with my client when I wasn't present.' She ignored Jenny's comments. 'I could have you on charges, or even have your badge for this.'

Jenny laughed aloud. 'It was a cup of tea over a few friendly words. I didn't ask a question. Not one. You can ask your client yourself. Or better still, check back on our security footage if you really need to.'

Jenny sauntered down the hall, past the room Penny was using for a lab and on into the main office area. It was then she finally relaxed, taking a long slow, steadying breath.

'How'd you go?' O'Connell kept his voice low.

'Miss fancy-pants turned up about two minutes too soon, but I could tell Rachel was flustered when I said Curtis could be in trouble and he could be the next murder victim.'

'Give her some time. We'll see if she flicks the lawyer or not.' O'Connell began packing up his desk for the night.

'I think Ms Hayes will be drumming into her exactly how quiet she needs to be. My chance might have flown out the window. What I don't get is why Rachel is letting Hayes represent her when she's obviously petrified of the woman?'

'Everyone is probably scared of that woman!'

Was that it? Was the lawyer simply intimidating? Jenny's instincts told her it was something else.

'Tomorrow is another day.' O'Connell pulled her out of her daydream with a gentle tap on her shoulder on his way past. 'I'll let Hayes know she has fifteen minutes to finish up or I'll lock her in for the night.'

Jenny laughed aloud as O'Connell disappeared down the back toward the cells. Her mind focussed on the counter computer. Wiggling the mouse, the computer sprang to life. Philips finished compiled the mobile phone videos and pictures from the BnS they gathered earlier.

A file sat on the desktop. She clicked it, only to find over two hundred little movie icons and at least a thousand thumbnail sized photos pop up on the screen. It would take all night to get through them.

O'Connell returned to the office. 'She didn't look happy.'

'I bet she didn't.' She turned back to the computer, a thought popping into her head unbidden. 'Hey Sir, if I copy these files, is it okay for me to take them home to view them?'

O'Connell frowned. 'Sure, but don't you have something more interesting to do?'

'Not really. I've hit a stall point with my other personal cases. I might as well get this one stowed away. Then maybe I can grab a few days off and do a little more investigating.

A large photo icon caught her eye. She opened the file and whistled. 'That sounds promising.'

'It certainly is.' She opened the photo to full screen. A two second glance was all she got.

'You need to release my client. Her bail has been approved.' Hayes waltzed into the main office passing behind Jenny. She flicked the computer back to the home page, but not before Hayes caught a glimpse.

The lawyer placed paperwork on the counter in front of Jenny. 'I'll take her with me now.' Jenny's stomach did a summersault. Something in Hayes's eyes made her nervous.

'I'll bring her out, but I think we should offer her protective custody, don't you?' Hayes flinched. 'She is still a material witness in a murder investigation.'

'That sounds like a good idea.' O'Connell stepped forward. 'By the way Ms Hayes, has Curtis turned up yet?'

'Not that I'm aware of.' Hayes smiled, without warmth. 'As her lawyer, I need to be aware of Rachel's whereabouts at all times.'

'If she continues to have you as her counsel, I'll be sure to notify you.'

Chapter 18

Jenny glanced at her watch as she yanked her backpack from her locker. Gazing over her shoulder, she checked to see if the USB drive was finished downloading the video and photo file.

O'Connell swung a set of keys around his finger. 'Are you done?' 'Just need to grab this memory card, then I'm out of here.'

'Any plans?'

'I was going to meet Penny at the motel, but I'll take Rachel home to my place for the night. I think I can convince her I can protect her and then she might waive her counsel.'

'Are you sure? You're not authorised to carry your duty weapon.'

'I'm better than nothing. Rachel knows something. A lot more than she's telling us. Was it her purse or Melinda's? Why would someone steal it from the crime scene? If it was Hayes, she got Jake to give up Melinda's identity, so it wasn't to hide who she was. Something must have been in that purse.'

'Just be careful, and don't work on those photos all night.'

'I won't.' Jenny retrieved the drive, powered down the computer and strode out to the cells. The door was open, Rachel still sitting inside.

'Do you have somewhere to stay tonight?'

'I'm fine.'

'Then why are you still here? I can offer you protection Rachel. I told you that before.'

The woman sighed, then collected the belongings O'Connell returned to her after bail was posted.

'Look, I won't ask you questions if you don't want me to, but you and I both know you don't want Hayes representing you.'

'I need to speak with Nigel Smart.' Rachel was close to tears again.

'Come back to my place. It's safe. You can trust me Rachel. Sleep in my bed tonight and hopefully we can get a hold of Smart tomorrow. You sure you don't want me to organise a flight home for you?'

Her eyes widened. Her head shook from side to side. 'Maybe I can trust you, but I don't feel safe anywhere right now. Locked up here seems best.'

But she wasn't locked up. The cell was open. The bed uncomfortable. She was either petrified of something or wanted to be left alone. Either option wasn't good.

'Look, you are free to go wherever you want, but if you are afraid of someone, you should tell me who. I can protect you. We can protect you.'

Rachel was lost in thought, then she sucked in a quick breath. 'Okay. I'll stay at your place tonight, but it's important I speak with Smart.'

'We'll try again tomorrow. Okay?' Rachel nodded; Jenny led her outside. Collecting her mobile from her backpack on the way, she texted Penny she wouldn't make it to dinner and drinks.

Her phone buzzed a second later. She answered the call as she turned out the lights and pulled the station door closed.

The beginnings of a glorious sunset lit the sky. Heat was coming off the day and the desert crispness filled the air.

'Hi. Sorry to blow you off. I'm on guard duty.'

'You have to eat.' Jenny could hear voices in the background. Nev and Tim called out. 'Come on Jenny.' Then she heard another voice, giving her goose bumps, the good kind. 'Nick is here. Nev invited him.'

'Damn. I have to take Rachel to my place. Can you explain?'

'Okay, I'll grab takeaway and meet you there.'

'That would be awesome. I've got video footage and photos to go through. I could use your help. Bring your laptop.'

Penny sighed. 'Don't you ever stop working!'

Jenny laughed, but stopped when she saw Rachel's expression. 'Hey, I need to go. See you soon.'

She scanned the area around her rusty Dodge, tension rose in her neck and shoulders. 'What's up Rachel?'

'Nothing.' Her voice quivered.

Jenny decided now wasn't the time to push, instead, she put her arm behind Rachel instinctively, steering her gently toward the passenger's side of her vehicle.

Rachel glanced nervously over her shoulder as Jenny opened the door. 'Get in.' She knew she sounded anxious. She was. Someone was watching them. Rachel could sense it too. Would they follow her home?

'My friend Penny is picking up dinner. It will probably be pasta – she knows I love pasta.' Jenny kept her voice as calm as possible as she climbed into the driver's seat, keys already in her hand. 'She's a forensic police officer. You'll like her.'

Rachel's long hair tossed from side to side as she rapidly scanned over her shoulder. 'I'm only fifteen minutes from here. We'll be there in no time.'

Rachel's eyes were wide, distracted. Jenny started the car, pushed the column-shift into drive and carefully pulled out of the carpark. Her wheels still spun on the gravel; the sound made Rachel jump.

The woman was wound tighter than a ball of string. Whatever she knew. Whatever got Melinda killed was now keeping Rachel tight-lipped, but it wasn't going to save her. Talking would be her only chance. Now Jenny only needed to convince her.

Chapter 19

Jenny's eyes were gritty, but she wasn't giving up. Glancing at her watch she realised over an hour of scouring through photos and footage yielded nothing new. She watched her bedroom door intermittently.

Rachel was a bundle of nerves, but a hot shower and food seemed to settle her.

She pushed to her feet. Her vision swam. Grabbing the kitchen breakfast bar, she steadied herself. 'I'll grab some water. Do you want one?'

Penny didn't comment, her eyes were glued to her laptop screen. Jenny filled two glasses with ice, then added water. What she desperately wanted was coffee, but it wasn't a good idea this late at night. As desperate as she was to stay awake and find video or more photos of the tattooed guy, she wasn't willing to ruin what little chance of sleep she might have later.

'I'm not sure we're going to find what you're looking for, as easily as you'd hoped.' Penny watched another digital phone video from the BnS ball, in triple time.

'Stop! What's that?' Jenny put the glasses down on the dining room table next to Penny's laptop. 'Rewind it.'

Penny rewound while the video played. 'There!' Jenny pointed.

'Where?' Penny watched the video play back at regular speed, her eyes focussed, her brow creased.

'There.' Jenny pointed to the background of the footage. 'That's Curtis and the guy with the tattoos.'

'Are you sure?'

'I'm sure. Go back a bit more. It's only a quick glimpse, but…' Jenny waited to explain until Penny started the video again.

'I see it.' Penny slowed the footage down. 'He doesn't look happy.'

'Curtis?'

'Either of them. Wait up, I saw him at the pub before you called. That's the same leather lace-up vest he was wearing tonight.'

'When?'

'Just before you called. He was talking with Hayes. I didn't pay too much attention.'

'That can't be a coincidence. We need to get a copy of any video footage Marj might have. I'll chase it up tomorrow. Can you zoom in on this?' Jenny fidgeted impatiently.

'I'm a forensic scientist, not a bloody IT expert. Wrong department Jen.'

'Damn. I'm okay with computers, but I couldn't edit a video if my life depended on it.'

'You and me both.'

'We need to find more footage. Between this argument and when Melinda was killed.'

'You think this guy killed her?'

'I'm thinking it's possible. You saw him with Hayes. I think she stole the purse from the scene, I just can't prove it yet. He could have torched the truck too.' Jenny slid into the chair in front of her own laptop and wriggled her finger over the mouse pad until it sprang to life. 'What time is it in that video?'

'Around ten. The band must have been on a break.' Penny peered over her laptop screen as Jenny nodded.

'Yeah. A DJ played for about half an hour between sets.'

'Did you notice where all the band members were then?'

'No. Nev had me squeezed between him and a seething pit of cowboy hats and boots on the dance floor.'

'I wish I'd seen that.' Penny grinned.' You and all those hot bods.'

'It wasn't pretty. Two guys nearly knocked me over, one stepped on my toe and my boots won't come clean from all the beer slopped onto them. Why on earth do people need to hold a beer on the dance floor?'

'It's Australian. I'm sure people don't do it overseas.' Penny closed the file they'd watched and placed it in a separate folder.

'I think we can search these files by date and time somehow.' Jenny squinted at the screen.

'I might not be an IT expert, but I can do that. What are you thinking?' Penny drank her water and sat back in her chair.

'I'm thinking we nail down any video taken between the argument and the murder. Maybe we'll get lucky?'

'That could still take the rest of the night.'

Jenny pushed back her chair and stood. A wicked grin crossed her face. 'It's not coffee, but I think it might give us the pick-me-up we need without ruining the few hours of sleep we might get later.'

She scurried to the fridge before Penny could guess what she planned. A few seconds later, she waved a large family block of chocolate in the air. Penny laughed, but Jenny wasn't done yet. She opened the freezer and produced a small tub of Cookies and Cream ice-cream. A few more steps and she pulled two teaspoons from the top drawer, bringing the spoils to the dining table.

'A woman after my own heart.' Penny picked up a spoon, as Jenny pulled the top from the ice-cream container with a loud pop. They giggled quietly, hushing each other so they didn't wake anyone.

'Now you know why I love caramel syrup in my coffee.'

Chapter 20

The advantage of living in a dugout was that there was only one way in and one way out. That meant there was no way Rachel could sneak out overnight without going past her, but it was also a fire evacuation nightmare if a pyromaniac set the place alight.

The fire extinguisher toppled over as Jenny flung her sleeping bag to the living room floor. Light filtered through the lonely front window. Reaching for her watch, Jenny confirmed the time. Six a.m. was too early.

Her mouth tasted like day-old fairy floss, with the sticky texture to match. It was three a.m. before they finally called it a night. Penny drove back to the motel. Jenny fell asleep on the lounge, exhaustion taking over.

Standing, she tip-toed her way to the bathroom, then almost laughed aloud. The sandstone floors didn't creak like her old farmhouse wooden floors back home. She could have run to the loo with clogs on and no one would have heard her.

Finishing in the bathroom, she stopped by her bedroom door. Cracking the door, Jenny peaked inside. It was a waste of time. With no lights on and no window, the place was pitch black.

Sighing, she dawdled through the lounge room to the small kitchen bench where her laptop was on charge. Three files sat on her desktop. She transferred them back to the USB and put it in her backpack.

It was at least another hour before she needed to wake Rachel. She opened her social media account. Personally, not a fan, but everyone was jumping on board and they were often sharing their entire lives, without any thought of privacy. This was the first time she thought of checking out Melinda's and Rachel's profiles.

Both women travelled in socialite circles, so they likely posted regularly. A quick tap of the keys brought up Melinda's profile. The petite blonde's profile picture appeared professional, but a quick browse through her album proved Melinda Smart always looked fabulous in public.

There was nothing damning, or overly interesting in the women's social circle. The usual private school friends. The expected events with pretty dresses and champagne flutes.

Giving up on Melinda, Jenny typed in Rachel Bridges. Two profiles with the same name popped up, one with the initial A. Clicking it, Jenny found Rachel Anne Bridges did indeed have a social media profile.

Scrolling through the photos, Jenny found plenty with Melinda, at the same events. On the edge of frustration and fed up with looking at fancy clothing and expensive jewellery, Jenny closed the photos and read Rachel's bio.

Rachel's file showed three employment records, including her most recent. Jenny's mouth gaped open as she read the name of the firm. Snapping the laptop shut, she stood, pacing back and forth, wondering if she should haul Rachel out of bed right now.

She wanted to take her down to the station and put some pressure on her, with O'Connell or Philips to witness, but she might call Hayes back in out of desperation, which was the last thing she wanted.

Damn, why didn't she check social media first? She should have thought of it. Without a warrant, they couldn't get her work history, but it was right there in full public view for the world to see – If only she'd looked.

'Hey. You're up early.' Nev wandered into the kitchen with his boxers on. 'Why didn't you put a light on?' He strolled sleepily to the kitchen wall and flicked the switch. His brown skin shone like bronze.

The guy was a hottie and he knew it. Ever since she played the friend's card, he was the perfect gentlemen. But now, even-though she was keen on Nick, she couldn't help but admire his abs.

'I didn't exactly sleep like a baby.' She gestured to the rumpled sleeping bag on the couch.

'Hey. You brought a guest home and stayed up most of the night working. Not me.' He shrugged his shoulders, palms up. 'Personally, I was expecting you to bring a guy home eventually, but another woman and not even sleeping in the same bed, well that totally ruined the fantasy.

'Oh shut up.' She was smiling, despite wanting to throw something at him. 'She's in danger. I had no choice.'

'You had a choice. You chose to be the great girl you are.' His gaze lingered a moment. Clearing his throat, he turned to the fridge. 'Do you want a cuppa?'

'No. I'll wait for Nikolic's.'

'I'm sure you go there for Niko more than the coffee.' The mischievous grin was back.

'I'll call the Fifth.'

'A shame we don't have a Fifth Amendment.' Nev winked. 'Toast?'

'That I can do. Thanks. I'll wake Rachel up. I need to get her through the shower first.'

'Good idea. Tim was on late shift. He'll be home soon and you know how long he spends in the shower after work.'

Jenny rolled her eyes skyward. 'Anyone would think we don't have a water shortage.' Opening her bedroom door, she felt for the light switch and turned it on. 'Rachel. Time to….' Rushing inside, searching the room. 'Rachel! Where are you?'

'Everything okay?' Nev called from the kitchen.

'Damn!'

Nev was by her side in a heartbeat. 'What?' He scanned the room, eyes wide and alert. 'She's gone. But how?'

'I crashed out when Penny left. I shouldn't have stayed up so late. She must have snuck right by me between three and six. Great guard I turned out to be.'

'Don't be too hard on yourself. If she's gone, it was of her own accord or we would all have woken up.'

'That's true.' Jenny picked up her mobile from the charger on her bedside. There was no signal and the screen was still locked. 'I need to get dressed and get to work. Sarge is going to be pissed.'

'She was on bail, right?'

'Yeah. But I was trying to get her to talk and keep her safe. Now whoever she feared, could find her and kill her like they did Melinda.'

'It was her choice to be here, so why leave?'

'Good point. I offered to put her on a plane home. She didn't want to. She kept asking to speak with Melinda's dad. I thought it was for legal advice, but maybe it was something else.'

'Where did she go then?'

'Your guess is as good as mine Nev.'

Chapter 21

Twenty minutes later she prepared herself for a long-winded explanation of how she lost a key witness in a murder investigation. Collecting the tray of coffees from her passenger seat, she slammed the door of her Dodge and rushed into the station.

'You look like crap.'

'Thanks. You say the nicest things.' Philips held his hand out for the coffee, but Jenny slapped it away. 'Actually. I'm not sure you deserve this.'

'Come on. You can't get a guy addicted, then deny him.' His whinge reminded her of her older brothers. They used to sound the same when she came home from school and made hot buttered toast and Vegemite for herself and not for them.

'In that case.' She handed him the coffee. 'Told you I'd convert you.'

'Yeah. Yeah.' He smiled, closed his eyes and inhaled the brew.

Sergeant Mackenzie and O'Connell entered, chatting quietly. Jenny held up two cups and they smiled like kids with candy.

'Nice work Williams. I knew you'd come in useful for something.' Sarge's tone was gruff but a smile flicked at the corner of his mouth.

'I'm afraid I'm just buttering you all up.' Three sets of eyes fell on her, coffee cups held to lips. 'Rachel snuck out last night, while I was sleeping on the couch and before you go off at me, I did find some evidence you might be interested in.'

She rushed on without taking a breath. 'Penny and I spent most of the night going over some footage from the BnS and…' She scanned around for the whiteboard.

'I'll put an APB out for Rachel in a minute. Don't keep us waiting Williams. What did you find?' O'Connell still hadn't touched his coffee.

Jenny saw the whiteboard inside Sarge's office and rushed to retrieve it. Wheeling it out, she pushed it up alongside O'Connell's desk, picked up the marker pen and began writing.

'O'Connell and I saw a photo from the BnS last night which got me scouring through the footage and photos until nearly three a.m.. That's why I slept too deep to notice Rachel leave.'

She placed a photo of the tattooed man she printed earlier at home, on the whiteboard. 'Penny saw the same guy talking with Hayes at the pub last night. This guy.' She pointed to the photo, placed directly below the photo of Melinda.

'Nice neck tats,' Philips offered. 'Bikie affiliated?'

'I'd say so. I'm running him through the database as soon as I fill you all in.'

'Get on with it then.' Sarge sculled the last of his coffee and tossed his cup into the bin next to O'Connell's desk. Jenny's eyes lingered on her coffee, but she was too wired to worry about drinking cold coffee.

'We also found a video, two actually. The first one was around ten p.m.. Curtis and this guy look like they were having a heated argument. Penny is organising the Adelaide lab to enhance the video as we speak.'

'And the second?' O'Connell prompted.

'The second shows the guy leaving, while the band are still playing.'

'Let me guess. Just before Melinda was set on fire.' O'Connell's cup joined her boss' in the bin.

'But that's totally circumstantial. He could have been going for a pee.' Philips said what Jenny already considered.

'I know. But number one, we need to know who he is, so we can interview him. He wasn't amongst the witnesses we spoke to Friday night.'

'And why the hell Curtis was arguing with him?' Sarge finished for her.

'Exactly Sir.'

'Alright, now run us through the lead up to Rachel disappearing last night.' O'Connell's comment reminded her how she mucked up.

'I'm sorry Sir. I was multi-tasking, trying to fit too much in when I should have been focussed on watching Rachel and talking to her about why she was running scared. Now we won't know.'

'Self-deprecation is unbecoming. Get over it Williams.' O'Connell's expression softened. Jenny forced her tense shoulders to relax. 'Did you see anything, anything that might have made her run? Curtis is missing. Did he contact her somehow?'

'Nothing came through holding.' Jenny closed her eyes for recall. A chill ran down her spine, reminding her of the same sensation last night. 'I got the feeling we were being watched when we left to go home last night.'

'Did you see Curtis? Anything strange?' O'Connell searched for triggers. Anything that might help her recall minor details seen subconsciously.

'No, but Rachel was frightened. She was fidgety in the car, before we even drove off. She couldn't stop flicking her head around, like something outside was spooking her.'

'Was she scared or maybe apprehensive?' O'Connell pushed gently.

Jenny replayed the scene in her mind. Visualising it like a replay. Rachel's expression could have been anxious, not afraid. Her eyes flung open. 'You think Curtis was watching us? He wouldn't have known I was going to take her to my place.'

'She didn't appear to be in a hurry to leave the station. Maybe she planned to leave last thing and get Curtis to pick her up, but you took her to your place instead.'

'That's plausible I guess. I made it hard for her to say no.'

'These hypotheses all rely on Curtis being alive, and safe. Why not leave Rachel in our care? O'Connell picked up the whiteboard marker and added a question mark, and the words scared, running, next to Rachel and Curtis on the whiteboard.

'Good question. Rachel is running from something. Maybe Curtis is helping her?' Jenny studied the murder board, her head was hurting from lack of sleep, coffee and too many unanswered questions.

'None of this explains why Melinda was murdered.' O'Connell rubbed his chin.

'No, but I also found out who owned the black sports car I saw Hayes get into at the motel yesterday. I thought the guy with the tattoos might own it, but it's a company car owned by Campbell, Newman and Smart.'

'How are we going to find out who is driving it?' Philips said.

'I've got an idea.' Jenny picked up the office phone on O'Connell's desk and dialled. 'Smart won't take my calls at home, I'll try his office now.' The call connected. 'Good morning. I'd like to speak with Mr Smart please.'

'May I ask who is calling?'

'Constable Williams from Coober Pedy Police.'

'I'll put you through to his PA.'

Jenny went to protest, but the dial-tone told her she was being transferred whether she liked it or not. The phone rang three times.

'Mr Smart's office, Tracey speaking.'

'Hi Tracey. I'm Constable Williams from the Coober Pedy Police station. I'm investigating Mr Smart's daughter's death. I'd like to ask him some questions but I haven't managed to reach him yet.'

'I'm sorry but Mr Smart isn't taking calls.'

'Is Mr Smart at the office at all?' Jenny decided to take another tack. Would the man kill his own daughter? She hoped not.

'He's in bereavement, home with his wife.'

'I understand. I'll try and contact him there again. Can I speak with Mr Campbell instead?'

'He's busy with clients. I can pass your details on to his PA and he can call you back.'

'So he's in the office today?'

'Yes. Of course. With Mr Smart off, he's been busy all week.'

'And Mr Newman?'

'Mr Newman is retired. He works from home on occasion, consulting for the firm.'

'Thank you Tracey. You've been very helpful. Oh, you don't happen to have Mr Newman's home number?'

'I probably shouldn't give it out.' Jenny heard the hesitation.

'It might help us find the person who killed Melinda Smart.'

She shared the number. 'I hope you catch whoever did that to poor Melinda.'

'You were friends?'

'Yes, with Rachel too. She must be devastated.'

'She is. You work with Rachel then?'

'Not directly. She's Ms Hayes' PA.'

Jenny couldn't believe her luck. 'We'll find whoever killed Melinda. Thanks for your help. If Mr Campbell can ring me, that would be great.'

'I'll make sure his PA passes the message on.'

'Thank you.'

Chapter 22

'Sir. That was Mr Smart's PA. I checked out Rachel's social media last night and discovered she works for Campbell, Newman and Smart, but Smart's PA just confirmed Rachel is Hayes's PA.'

Sergeant Mackenzie was one step from his office door. He turned, 'You could have lead with that earlier.'

'Sorry Sir. So much happened last night. I have Newman's number too. I'll call his home now.'

Sarge scowled at O'Connell, then her. 'We need to bring that whiteboard up to date. I'm losing track of all the leads.'

'You call, I'll write, Williams.' O'Connell picked up the marker pen again, added the registration number of the vehicle, the name of the company and Rachel's work details to the board.

'Sounds like Hayes and the tattoo guy are looking better and better for this, but we still don't have motive.' Jenny picked up the office phone again, dialling Newman's home number.

'Newman residence.' A stoic female voice answered with a distinctly posh, British accent.

'Mrs Newman?'

'Yes.' Not a hint of curiosity in the woman's reply.

'I'm wondering if I can speak with your husband? Is he home?'

'I'm sorry. I didn't catch your name.'

'Of course. I'm Constable Williams, from the Coober Pedy Police. I just have a few questions. We're investigating the death of….'

'Poor Melinda of course.' The voice stepped up an octave, now filled with emotion. 'I'll fetch him for you dear.' The sound of muffled voices followed.

'This is Clint Newman.' Formal but polite.

'Mr Newman. I'm Constable Williams, from the Coober Pedy Police. I need to follow up on a few things and wondered if you might help me?'

'Of course. What do you need? Melinda was a gem.' Jenny could hear mixed emotions in the man's voice. Fondness and sadness in equal measure. 'I've known her, knew her, all her life.' His voice hitched.

'Sir. Do you know Samantha Hayes very well?' Jenny kept her tone neutral.

'A little. She started with the firm a few years ago. Smart employed her after I semi-retired so I've not had much to do with her. Why?'

Typical lawyer. Always on the defence. 'She's been here, representing the country rock band that were playing the night of Melinda's death.'

'She's defending one of the suspects?' His reply was outraged.

'Not at all Sir. The band members are all cleared of any wrongdoing in Melinda's death. They were merely helping with our enquiries.'

'Then why did they need a lawyer?'

He's quick!

'They were initially brought in for questioning because one of the band members is known to the victim. And there were other possible charges but they are all clear now. But Sir, that's not the reason for my call.'

'What is it then?'

'Hayes has been seen getting into one of your company cars here. But she arrived by plane, so the car is of interest to us.'

She tapped her pen lightly on the desk notepad and resisted the urge to chew the end.

'Which car?' Jenny noted the hesitation.

'A black Audi.' She gave him the registration number in case there were multiple metallic black Audis in the carpool.

Silence followed. Mr Newman cleared his throat. 'Exactly what has this vehicle got to do with Melinda's murder?'

'We aren't sure it has any connection Sir.' Jenny spoke slowly, trying to gauge the sudden change in Mr Newman's tone.

'I think you'll need to get a warrant before I can discuss this any further with you.'

'You know who's been driving the vehicle? Is it Mr Smart?'

'I'm afraid I can't help you without a warrant.'

'Someone brutally murdered Melinda Smart Sir.' She knew this was her last chance to get him to tell her what she needed to know. 'By not giving us the information, you could effectively be protecting a murderer. Don't you want to see justice?'

She gave it all she could. A long, agonising silence was broken by exactly what she didn't want to hear.

'Good day Constable.' The line went dead.

Chapter 23

Jenny glanced up to see O'Connell staring at her. She shook her head slowly and placed the handset on the cradle.

'What did you expect from a lawyer?'

'He asked me to get a warrant before he could share who has been driving the Audi.' She still couldn't get her head around his sudden change in attitude.

'He likely knows who it is then.'

'Yes! And wants to protect them.'

'I've organised for a St Kilda patrol to head around and check Smart is home as his PA claimed.'

'That's something I guess. But if we eliminate Smart, who else could be driving the car?
Campbell is working in Melbourne, Newman answered his home phone number.'

'Are there any other junior partners? The place would have para-legals, PA's, secretaries. Any other staff who aren't accounted for?'

'I could call Tracey back, but why would Newman protect a junior partner or other staff member?' She sighed.

'His reputation.' O'Connell sounded even less convinced than Jenny was.

'I don't think so Sir. It's easy to distance yourself from a rogue employee. Just sack them.' She undid her ponytail, smoothed her auburn hair and retied it. 'I'm guessing closer to home than that.'

'We better run his family, but before we do, I'd like another chat with Jake, Scott and Blake.
They must have some idea where Rachel and Curtis are, and why they have gone missing.'

'Maybe they know why Curtis was fighting with the tattoo guy?'

'And where Rachel might be?'

'Hopefully. Philips, you go with Williams.'

'On it Sarge.' They collected their weapons and left the station. The sun belted down, promising another hot day in the arid desert opal mining town. Jenny pushed her Akubra hat firmly on her head and joined Philips crossing the road to the motel.

When she came to Coober Pedy, she expected it to be warm, but she never thought it would be scorching enough to fry an egg on the bonnet of her car. Arriving to start her new job in January was a baptism of fire. Then flooding rain washed the place out, leaving the roads in need of repair even now, a month later.

Sweat was already beading on her forehead as she strode down the covered veranda, to the motel bar and restaurant. They opened the glass doors, did a quick recognisance of the room and quickly discovered the band wasn't in the dining room eating breakfast.

'If you do a walk by the units, I'll go see if I can get the room numbers from Marj.'

'Sounds like a plan.' Philips wandered down the rear walkway as Jenny hurried to Reception. A pedestal fan rustled papers on the front counter, while the television played a US daytime soap quietly in the background and Marj sat in her usual spot, behind the counter, a mystery novel in her hand.

'Hey Marj.' The full busted redhead had put a pink rinse through her hair. Her face lit up before Jenny spoke. 'Have you seen Samantha Hayes or the boys from the band this morning?'

The smile dropped away at the mention of the city lawyer. The woman had that effect on Jenny but she said nothing. 'Ms Hayes checked out. I don't think any band members were staying here. What were the names?'

Jenny frowned. 'Curtis Greenfield, Jake Masters? Scott or Blake, can't recall their last names off the top of my head.'

Marj pursed her lips and shook her head. 'Nope. They never checked in here.'

'Damn. They gave this as their address.' Marj's first answer sunk in. 'You said Ms Hayes has checked out.'

'Yes. This morning. Proof there is a God.' She raised her hands to the sky and grinned wickedly.

Jenny didn't wait. If the lawyer was gone and the band members weren't at the motel as they claimed, then they might all be skipping out of town.

'Thanks Marj.' She turned to rush out the door on the carpark side, but stopped and turned back. 'Nice tint.' Not waiting for a response, she took off looking for her partner.

'Philips!' she called across the back-parking lot when she spotted him knocking on doors. He turned to the sound of her voice. 'Lets' go!' She waved him over.

He jogged across the gravel as she let her mind wander. Why would they run? Unless they were involved with Melinda's death?

'What's up?' Philips wasn't sweating. She wished she stayed that cool in the heat. 'Marj said Hayes checked out this morning and the band members never checked in.' Philips screwed up his nose. 'What do you think that means?'

'I'm not sure. But if Samantha Hayes is leaving town, we've got to be asking why.' Philips fell into step alongside her as they rushed back toward the station.

'She's not under any obligation to stay, right?'

'Right, but why has she pulled out on the guys? Why was she even here to start with? Did you ever confirm she was on that flight?'

'Only on paper. Why?'

'Because we need to speak to Hayes about who is driving that black Audi. If she arrived in the car, not on the plane, she jumps to the top of our suspect list.' Jenny picked up the pace, jogging across the road. 'Let's go.'

'Where?'

'We'll try the airport first.' Jenny glanced at her watch. 'If they booked a flight, the first one out is due to leave in about thirty minutes.'

'I'll grab the keys, you tell the boss.'

'Chicken.' Jenny joked.

'You bet I am.'

Jenny slowed down as she entered the station. Penny turned when she saw them. 'Hey. I thought you were bringing back coffee.'

'No time to explain.' She rushed past her friend at the front counter, lifted it and ducked inside in one smooth motion.

'About the coffee.' Penny sounded perplexed. 'What's going on?' She quizzed Philips as he rushed to collect his keys.

'Sir?' O'Connell and Sarge called out in unison from the back office. Jenny didn't make out their words, but it didn't matter. They were together which made explaining easier.

She pushed the door open, hurried inside, and stopped, her mouth hanging open. Sitting in her Hot Seat, as she'd come to know the Sergeant's extra chair, was the last person she ever expected to see there.

'Williams. Meet Detective Roberts.'

She couldn't think straight. She couldn't close her mouth either, but words wouldn't come out.

'Sir?' She finally found her voice as her eyebrows lowered into a deep frown.

Turning around to face her, Tattoo-Man smiled and Jenny's stomach did a backflip. She was ready to string him up for murder no less than twenty minutes ago. Now she was back to square one.

Chapter 24

The detective rose smoothly, wiped his hands on his torn denim jeans and extended his right hand in greeting.

'Constable Williams. I've heard good things about you.' Heat rose to her cheeks. She hoped she wasn't blushing.

She cleared her throat, her thoughts fluttered around like a butterfly in spring. She couldn't find words. Thankfully O'Connell filled the gap.

'Detective Roberts came in a few minutes ago. He was just briefing us.'

Visions of the girl from the Exorcist flashed in her mind. Was her head spinning around and around like a demon? Her thoughts were.

She finally shut her mouth. 'Thank you, Sir.' She shook his extended hand, aware she left it hanging in the air too long. 'Can someone please tell me what the hell is going on?'

Philips stuck his head around the corner. 'Are we going?' His mouth hung open exactly like hers did a moment before. 'Ah!'

'Sir. We need to check the airport. Hayes has checked out. We need to question her about,' she squinted at the detective, 'you know.'

Sarge's eyes flicked to Roberts, then back. 'Leaving town isn't a crime Williams.' 'No Sir. But the band members aren't at the motel. They never were.'

'I know.'

'You know?' Philips said what she was thinking before she could. His face was a mirror image of what she probably looked like.

'You know where they are?' she huffed.

'Detective Roberts here does.' Sergeant Mackenzie waved a hand at Roberts who stood alongside the desk, his arms across his chest, his muscled tattoos flexing.

She hesitated. A thought popped into her mind and jumped out of her mouth before she could stop it. 'We've checked him out. Right!'

The detective chuckled. 'I like her.' He glanced between O'Connell and Sarge.

'I'm so glad.' She didn't hold back her sarcasm. The initial shock of her prime suspect turning into a cop was wearing off.

'We could find a spot for her in Melbourne.'

'You can't have her.' O'Connell and Sarge spoke in unison. Her cheeks flushed.

'Fair enough,' he shrugged casually.

'Will someone please answer my question? Do I try and catch Samantha Hayes?'

All eyes fell to Detective Roberts. Had they checked him out! She still didn't have a definitive answer.

'Hayes hasn't skipped town yet.' Roberts assured her.

'Stand down you two. I'll brief you once we've finished with the detective here.'

'Yes Sarge, but where are the band members? We've still got a murder to investigate.' And two missing witnesses. She wasn't giving up yet. Roberts' smile made her stomach churn. Was it a nervous flutter? Or was it her instincts screaming at her that something wasn't right?

****

Penny was still waiting in the front office when Jenny closed Sergeant Mackenzie's door. Philips' face said he wanted to rant as much as she did, but now wasn't the time to air their grievances.

'What on earth is going on?' Penny's hands were on her hips, her need for coffee totally forgotten.

'Apparently, we have an undercover cop and he's Tattoo Man.'

'No way!' Penny's eyes bulged.

'Yes way!' A thought struck her. 'Did you see Samantha Hayes, the lawyer this morning at the motel?'

'At breakfast, no. I saw her get into a metallic black sportscar when I left the restaurant though. I think it was an Audi, but I only got a quick glimpse of the back end.'

'An Audi.' Jenny repeated. She'd assumed it was Tattoo…she had to stop calling him that now she knew he was a detective. But if it wasn't Roberts, who was it?

She scurried over to O'Connell's desk. He was a creature of habit and like Sarge, printed out everything he was working on.

'What are you doing?' Penny followed her.

'I'm checking to see if O'Connell has managed to get a report we were talking about yet.'

'What report?' Philips asked as he stepped up alongside Penny. They hung over her shoulder like two crows as she lifted every piece of paper, then sighed.

'He hasn't. Damn.' She sat down at the computer and checked the Births, Deaths and Marriages portal for a report request on Mr Newman and his wife.

'What are you doing?' Philips watched her fingers typing.

'Penny saw Hayes get into a black Audi this morning. I ran the registration earlier, after talking to O'Connell. It is registered to Hayes's firm but if she came by plane, who drove it? Newman got all antsy when I questioned him about the car. He knows who is driving it but wouldn't tell me.'

'So you want to know if he has any relatives?' Penny observed the details.'

'Yes, but I can't get the details until the report Sarge lodged comes back, which could take another day.'

Penny's face lit up. 'I might know someone.' Jenny waited as Penny lifted the desk phone and dialled.

'Mack. Sweety. I'm in Coober Pedy. Yes I know. Back of nowhere.' A voice nattered on, muffled by the earpiece. 'Except for Pricilla, yes of course.' Penny rolled her eyes. Jenny stifled a giggle. 'Can you please be a darling and run a check for me? And email it through?'

Jenny scribbled down the email for the station as Penny explained what she needed, then read out the email details.

'Perfect. Bye Darl.' She hung up, tapped the computer screen in front of Jenny and grinned. 'Should be in any second.'

'Who?' Penny put up her hand.

'Can't tell you or I'll have to kill you.' Philips snorted. 'No. Honestly. Mack and I go way back. I'll give him your details in case you need help next time. He's usually pretty good unless it's something sensitive.'

An emailed pinged on the server. Jenny rushed to open it up.

'The Newman's registered two births, Mathew and Michael. But...' She read on. 'Apparently Mathew has since died. Surviving son is Michael. I'll run him through police records.'

A file popped up, which shocked her. The son of a top lawyer with a police record. She shook her head. Her pulse ramped up as she opened the file, scanning it carefully for anything pertinent to her investigation.

He was ex-army, retired, now working as a fire and safety officer for one of the largest mining companies in the country. The police record didn't have his service details.

'He could be our arsonist.' Penny tapped the screen. 'Look, fire and safety.'

'We'll need to get a hold of his army records. He could have been involved with explosives in the army.'

'He could be our driver.' Philips shifted from one foot to the other. 'But we still need to find Hayes.'

'She was on the manifest. Let's make sure she got on the plane. Then we might be able to confirm if she or Michael Newman were driving the Audi.'

Philips rushed to the desktop computer. 'I'll request copies of the airport security footage.'

'I'll search to see if Michael Newman has a vehicle registered in his name.'

'I'd like to know why he has a police record. Open that first.' Penny nudged Jenny's arm.

She flicked back to the police record and read on. Penny tapped her arm firmly. 'I'm getting there.' She heard Sarge's office door open.

Sergeant Mackenzie cleared his throat. Jenny glanced up, then turned to Penny who shrugged with a look saying I tried to get your attention.

'You have something to share Williams?' Sergeant Mackenzie raised an eyebrow. O'Connell grinned at her discomfort.

'Nothing concrete Sir. As soon as I'm sure, you'll be the first to know.' She eyed the detective, whose grin said he was mildly amused by her lack of transparency.

Chapter 25

Jenny gave Philips a warning glare. He frowned with confusion, then his eyes went wide as Roberts approached the counter near the computer he was searching on. Flicking the mouse, he cleared the screen. Jenny only hoped it was before Roberts saw.

She reverted the Senior Constable's computer screen to the home page and stood. Clearing her throat, she spoke, her eyes fixed on Roberts and his stupid grin. 'So are we bringing in the band to interview them again Sir?'

'We need to make sure our investigation doesn't interfere with Detective Roberts's first Williams. Leave it be a minute hey?' O'Connell was toeing the line.

'Thanks for your cooperation and I'm sorry I didn't check in earlier guys. It's just this case is five years in the making. I've been working with the Harlequins the whole time. Getting this rank in the gang hasn't been easy. Even coming in here is a huge risk.'

'So why did you?' Sergeant Mackenzie and O'Connell turned to glare at her in eerie unison. They wanted him out, and her to shut up. *Keep quiet!* She grumbled to herself.

He chuckled without missing a beat. 'Because you are a bloody good investigator and you're at risk of blowing me out of the water Williams.'

Was he legitimate? Was she getting too close and it might blow his cover? 'So Melinda's death doesn't matter?'

'It certainly does matter, but this is huge Constable. This case has the potential to bust the Harlequin drug trade wide open, and the gang are connected. I want all the loose ends tied up before we bust them.'

'Just legalise the shit and we can all go home.' Penny's arms were tight across her chest, her square jaw set hard.

'I hear this argument all the time and I don't have time to debate it with you now. But I'd like to sometime Ms McGregor.'

He knows Penny. I hope he's on the up and up.

The forensic scientist smiled in a way Jenny was too familiar with. The girl was a loose cannon and she loved bad boys. 'I might take you up on that offer Detective.' She inclined her head in mock challenge.

'I look forward to it.' He saluted the Sergeant and shook O'Connell's hand before leaving without further conversation.

The entire team watched silently, all visibly holding their breath until he left the building. A tense mood hung in the air as everyone realised the case was just taken out of their hands. But Jenny hoped her boss wasn't ready to give up easily.

'Hayes is off limits, but the band are clear to question.' The corners of her mouth subconsciously turned into a grin as Sarge barked out orders. 'Williams. You and Philips go get them from the caravan park, O'Connell has the details.'

Jenny thought about Michael Newman's police record. Should she tell her boss now? She got into so much trouble last time she kept case information to herself. But Sarge just told her Hayes was off limits. That wasn't what she wanted to hear. Hayes and Newman were connected and Philips was working on confirming if the lawyer boarded the plane or not.

'We'll bring the band members in Sir.' Jenny turned to leave.

'Detective Roberts confirmed Curtis isn't with the band. I'll add him to the APB I put out on Rachel.' O'Connell spoke as Sergeant Mackenzie returned to his office.

'How does Detective Roberts even know the band?' Jenny resisted the urge to put her hands on her hips.

'He wasn't at liberty to say. That is a direct quote by the way.' O'Connell smiled as Jenny rolled her eyes.

'Ok. I've heard enough. Time to go.' She tapped Philips on the shoulder on her way out.

****

Jenny knocked on the caravan door and waited in the hot, early autumn sun. The caravan park boasted two tall gumtrees, red dirt as far as the eye could see and a host of onsite vans that might have barely survived World War Two.

The smell of stale beer wafted in her face as the internal door of the van swung open. The dark mesh made it difficult to see who greeted her, but by the height, Jenny guessed it was the lead guitarist Scott Cuthbertson.

'What!'

'Scott, isn't it?' Scott's tone set the hairs on her neck on alert. Her hand rested on her hip belt, close to her firearm and Taser.

'Who the hell is it?' Jake's voice was unmistakable, even though it sounded like his vocal cords where strained. His unique, high pitched speaking voice didn't match his singing voice.

'Jake. It's Constables Williams and Philips. Our Sergeant wants another word with all of you at the station.'

'Rack off. It's been a shitty few days.' Jake appeared behind Scott, the mesh still providing a barrier.

A waft of smoke drifted toward Jenny. The reason for the delay tactics became obvious.

'I smell cannabis. Don't you?' She turned to Philips who raised his nostrils to the door and sniffed loudly.

'Yep. I think I do. You boys are going to have to open up.'

'This is private property. You can't search private property without consent or a search warrant.' The third band

121

member appeared, squeezing between Jake and Scott. Blake was a quiet guy with long curly jet-black hair.

'Here's the thing guys. You are renting this caravan from the park owner and old man Braithwaite has given us permission to enter, so you see your dilemma. Right!'

The third member disappeared. The sound of glass breaking made Jenny jump, but she laughed aloud when she heard the chemical toilet click open at the rear of the van.

'You do know you don't have a septic or sewage connected to the toilet now, don't you?' Jenny heard Philips snigger, making a straight face almost impossible to hold in place.

'Blake. Leave it mate.' Jake unlocked the black screen door as Scott shuffled aside to let him pass.

'Look, we don't need to search the premises if you all just do what we've asked. Sergeant Mackenzie has more questions we need you to answer. Have any of you seen Curtis? Or Rachel?'

Jake ambled down the fold-out aluminium stairs, his shoulders drooping in defeat. Scott followed a few steps behind. The tall guitarist's eyes scanned the carpark over Jenny's shoulder. She fought the urge to glance to where he was staring.

Stepping aside to allow the third member to exit the van, Jenny took the opportunity to glance through the rows of caravans, past the site office to the road beyond.

Parked a few metres from the entrance was a black Audi. The tinted windows made it impossible to see who was driving, but Jenny was certain wherever the car was, the owner and Hayes weren't far away.

She needed to get these guys out of plain sight and into the station before something happened.

'Come on guys. We'll give you a lift down to the station.'

'We can drive.' Jake protested, but Scott nudged him to look up. The singer's face paled. 'Maybe we'll grab a lift.' His colour didn't improve.

Philips frowned, but as he turned to their vehicle, he saw the black sports car backing out of a parking spot outside the park entrance.

'You guys know the owner of that car?' Philips asked, not taking his eyes from the vehicle. 'No! Why would we?' Jake's answer was rushed.

'You didn't even look to see which car I meant.' Philips pressed the unlock on his keys and waited with his hand on the door for an answer.

'I did.' Jake's tone was defensive. 'Just hurry up and get this over with will you.'

Jake reached for the door to the back seat, opened it and was inside before the black Audi pulled out of sight.

Chapter 26

Jenny led Jake to the interview room while Philips escorted Scott and Blake to the rear of the building – their eyes darting around nervously.

They were all rattled and it was Jenny's job to find out what they knew about the black Audi, its occupants and where Rachel and Curtis might be.

Jake sat at the interview table, hunched forward, his hand fidgeting on the surface. His nails were bitten to the quick, the cuticles red and raw. O'Connell entered, flicked the recording equipment on and pulled out a seat—the feet scraping loudly on the lino floor. He sat back, arms crossed over his chest, making it clear Jenny was leading the interview.

'Do you want your lawyer Jake?'

'No!' He steadied his breathing. 'Not right now, thanks.' He forced a relaxed tone.

'Do you have any idea where Curtis is?'

'I've already told you no.'

She shook her head, tutted, then thinned her lips and remained silent. It was a look she stole from her mum. It always worked on her. She hoped it would do the trick with Jake.

He sighed, visibly forcing his leg to stop tapping to an inaudible beat. 'I've not seen him since you last interviewed us all together and then we got the call to say the video footage he provided, backed up our story and we were free to go.'

'Okay. But you weren't free to leave town yet. He knew that, right?'

Jake shrugged.

'Help me understand a few things Jake.' Jenny smiled, trying to put the man at ease. She waited. He said nothing.

'Look Jake. How about I summarise what we know so far.' Jake shrugged. Jenny bit her lip to keep her frustration in check.

'This is what we know. Melinda was murdered. Your truck had enough methamphetamine in it to cause a massive explosion when someone lit it up and although you and your band members are in the clear for Melinda's murder, you used delay tactics, hindering our search of it before the explosion. Do you know anything about that Jake?'

He stayed silent.

O'Connell moved so unexpectedly, his hand slamming down on the interview table loud enough to make her ears ring. She jumped nearly as high as Jake.

'Stop stuffing around kid. Murder, accessory to murder. They all carry a heavy penalty and I'm not sure you're up to any jail time. Your sweet country sounds won't buy you a free pass, if you know what I mean. In fact, it might be considered sexy by some inmates.'

O'Connell's grin was malicious. She made a mental note to dig into his past and make sure she never got on his bad side.

'I didn't kill anyone. I've got nothing to do with any of this.' Jake whined.

'Come on lad. The drugs were in your band's truck.' O'Connell's face was inches from Jake's now. The singer sat back, trying to find some space, his cheeks red, his eyes wide.

'Tell us what you know and we can see what we can do on the drug charges.'

Jake gulped, opened his mouth as though he were about to speak, then stopped, his lips pressed together.

'What have they got on you?' Jenny could see he wanted to talk but for some reason, was unwilling. 'Have they threatened you?' O'Connell still loomed over the guy. His eyes darted from her back to O'Connell. His hands shook, then his head followed.

A firm knock on the door broke the tension. O'Connell swore under his breath. They were so close.

'Enter,' he grumbled.

Philips opened the door. 'Sorry Sir. Jake's lawyer is here.' Hayes barged right past the constable, but Jenny was ready for her.

She stepped between the interviewee and the lawyer, her hand up in front of her. 'I'm sorry Ms Hayes. We have it on record. Jake has refused counsel at this time.' The woman gaped. 'You'll need to respect his wishes and leave the interview room now.'

'That's coercion. I gave you express instructions not to interview any of the band members without me being present.' Her nostrils flared.

'And why is that Ms Hayes? Are you afraid of what they might reveal? Jake, Blake and Scott are all in protective custody, as of now. Leave or I'll arrest you.'

The lawyer scowled at everyone in the room one by one. Making sure to rest her acid stare on Jake before she pulled her shoulders back, turned and stomped from the room.

Jenny eased out a long slow breath, before smoothing her features and turning back to Jake. Moving forward, still standing, she placed her palms firmly on the desk and leant forward.

'Whatever you know, is going to get you killed just like Melinda. You've given us no choice but to place you into protective custody. You might as well give us what we need to nail that bitch and whoever she's working for because you're not going anywhere.'

Chapter 27

Jenny studied the whiteboard in the Sergeant's office, chewing her lip and the end of the marker pen in equal measure.

'What are you thinking Williams?' Sergeant Mackenzie sat behind his desk, his hands clasped, thumbs tapping together thoughtfully. O'Connell reclined comfortably in Sarge's Hot Seat. Maybe he'd never endured a grilling in that spot? Jenny's memory vividly recalled many heated lectures in her first few weeks on the job.

'Detective Roberts was seen arguing with Curtis. Penny is downloading the footage the techs managed to enhance. They even found a person who reads lips, so we might get a glimpse of the conversation. But what I'd really like to know is how an undercover cop – vice president of the Melbourne chapter of the Harlequins no less, ends up overseeing a drug lab and distribution in Coober Pedy, the back of nowhere. No offence.'

'None taken.' O'Connell smiled.

'But why doesn't Roberts see the need to blow the lid on the whole operation?'

'He said they were connected. You think he's dirty?' Sarge drummed his fingers on the desk, his face drilled hers.

'I don't know. He warned us off the lawyer, but not the band. Exposing the boys' involvement in drugs could blow the operation up for the Harlequins and his precious undercover job. So why let us at them?'

'Maybe he wants them blamed for all this? Keeps his cover from being compromised. He can tell his chapter he set them up to take the fall? A threat from the Harlequins will guarantee their silence or they'll die in prison.'

'Then who killed Melinda? It wasn't one of the boys. We know that.' Jenny's eyes remained fixed on the whiteboard.

'Rachel? She's on the run with Curtis,' O'Connell suggested. Jenny shook her head.

'Maybe she is an excellent actress, but Hayes frightened Rachel and you saw how Jake cringed when she stormed into the interview. Philips requested the airport footage, but they are dragging their feet. It would set my mind at ease that she didn't kill Melinda herself if she was on that plane.'

'What would the motive be?' Sarge waited as she studied the murder board.

'I don't think Melinda's death is drug related. Rachel is Hayes's PA. Maybe she got access to confidential files. Hayes represented Newman at his trial. He was cleared of all charges?'

'What charges?' Sarge glared at her. 'The whiteboard Williams. It's not on the whiteboard!'

'Sorry Sir, I tracked down Newman's son Michael's details while you were in the office with Roberts. He's got a police record, but I was interrupted when Roberts came out. I only checked back when we brought the band in for questioning.'

'What were the charges Williams?' O'Connell spoke quietly, trying to get her back on track.

'He was discharged from the army, then he worked in Afghanistan as a civilian contractor, but charges of arson were brought against him.'

'He might be nasty enough to kill to keep a secret, but what secret? Sarge stood and paced the room.

'I don't know Sir. I have a feeling Melinda wasn't the intended victim or if she was, Rachel is now the target. Hayes is the link. She knew the victim and Rachel is her PA. Rachel must know what the secret is. Have we gotten that warrant for Curtis' and Rachel's mobile phones yet?'

'No. The judge isn't convinced they are in danger and we have nothing to charge them with.'

'Maybe Penny's analysis of video footage will help us make up our minds about Curtis's involvement and where Roberts sits in all this. I could tell you were both sceptical about him when he was here. What else did he say when you spoke to him?'

O'Connell glanced at the Sergeant, who nodded his head. O'Connell ran his hand through his thick salt and pepper hair.

'He said he was in deep with the Harlequins. As Vice President, he was privy to a lot of what was going on, but if there was a drug lab in Coober Pedy it was news to him.'

'No way!' Jenny shook her head. 'If he wasn't here for drugs on behalf of the Harlequins, what was he here for? He must have known they were cooking Meth.'

'But we don't know they were.' Sarge was right. Jenny sighed. The swabs from the truck doors and a little trace of Meth in the purple purse weren't conclusive. Another accelerant might have caused the explosion.

'We asked him why he was in Coober Pedy and he said his reasons were confidential,' O'Connell added.

'That's a super cryptic reply. Let's say he's not here for drugs on behalf of the Harlequins, but Samantha Hayes is off limits, so she must be helping him with an investigation.' Jenny bit her lip, letting her mind mull over the details, trying to make sense of it.

'Go on.' O'Connell encouraged her to continue.

'We know the band didn't kill Melinda Smart and we can only link drugs to the band, so drugs weren't the motive.

That definitely puts us back with Melinda and Rachel knowing something about Hayes which got Melinda killed.'

'Let's see if the techs found what we need then.' Penny entered from the rear of the station, a USB stick in hand.

The Forensic Scientist stepped up to the Sergeant's desk. Smiling, she put her hand on his laptop. 'May I?' She didn't wait for an answer before swinging it around to face her. Inserting the memory stick into the slot, she began clicking buttons.

'Here. Watch this.' She queued the video, turned the screen so Sarge could still see it. Jenny and O'Connell huddled around the small laptop and waited. Penny pressed a few buttons, toggled up the volume and pressed play.

The close-up version of the video showed Roberts' tattoos clearly, but what surprised Jenny was the calm look on Curtis' face. Roberts was a scary guy with biceps as round as her thighs. Why wasn't the younger man intimidated?

Roberts pushed Curtis, who puffed up his chest and spoke. The words weren't audible, but captions appeared on the screen, added by the lip-reading technician.

"It's illegal, so they can pay up or quit."

Roberts' back was to the camera. No one caught his reply. Roberts pushed Curtis again, who pushed back. The situation was escalating, but the video showed Curtis keeping his head as another caption popped onto the screen.

'They better not,' was captioned, before the person with the camera scanned toward the dance floor.

'Curtis knew about illegal activities.' Jenny pushed back from the screen. 'Was he blackmailing Roberts for money?'

'Maybe it wasn't the boys dealing drugs, maybe he stumbled on Harlequin business.' Penny ejected the USB from the Sergeant's computer.

'That could certainly get whoever had the information, killed. But would Roberts do the killing? He likely stepped over the line already to make Vice-President.' Jenny's gut twisted at the thought of it. He was hiding something, she could tell, but that was what undercover cops did.

'At the bare minimum, it means Roberts hasn't been upfront with us.' Jenny nodded at the Sergeant's observation.

'What he said.' She pointed to her boss.

'But's he's an undercover detective. He doesn't owe us anything.' O'Connell pointed out. 'Maybe he doesn't. I asked the question and no one answered. Did we check him out?'

'I called his department in Melbourne. I spoke to his Sergeant who confirmed he is undercover, but he couldn't elaborate on where or what the case was.'

'All we've confirmed then is he's an undercover detective. Do his superiors know why he's in Coober Pedy? Do they know he's protecting Hayes?'

'I'll make a call.' He lifted the handset on his desk phone and shooed everyone out with the flick of his wrist.

Penny closed the door behind them and whispered. 'You think Roberts is dirty?'

'I think he's not telling us everything.'

Chapter 28

Philips slammed his locker closed. Jenny jumped.

'You're off with the fairies. What are you looking at?' Philips peered over her shoulder at the computer screen.

'Just downloading a few photos of Michael Newman. I might do a little canvassing tomorrow morning and see if anyone has noticed him around town.'

'I'll give you a hand.'

'Thanks. You go Philips. I'll finish up here. Where's O'Connell?' She scanned the office.

'O'Connell is doing first watch with the band tonight.'

'Where are they staying?'

Philips shrugged. 'No idea. It's need-to-know.' He tapped his nose like it was an espionage secret. Jenny rolled her eyes.

She pushed away from the desk, stepping to the locker to retrieve her own backpack. As she opened the door, her mobile rang. Glancing at the caller ID she frowned, but answered.

'Constable Williams speaking.'

There was a suspended silence, then background noise filtered through. Jenny could hear a dog barking and a newborn infant crying.

'I'm glad I got you.' The voice was breathless.

'Ms Clark. I'm glad you got me too.' Jenny tossed her backpack over her shoulder, pushed her phone between her chin and shoulder, then closed the locker.

'What's happened to Curtis?' The woman sounded worried. Ms Clark obviously hadn't seen her brother recently. 'He promised to be here for the baby's arrival.' The infant crying kicked up a notch. 'But he didn't make it.'

'I was hoping he was with you, but I'm sure he's just gotten side-tracked.' She added the latter too hastily

'I told him this would happen.' Her voice quivered.

'What do you mean?'

'He's always had his eyes on the top prize.' Jenny waited, but Curtis' sister wasn't giving more without a push.

'If you think Curtis is in trouble Ms Clark, I encourage you to help us make sure he's okay?'

'I spoke to him last week. He said he had something that would make us all rich.' She let out a loud breath. 'My ex is a pig. I'm going to raise this bub on my own and Curtis wanted to make sure we were okay.'

The baby's cries were a high-pitched wail now. Ms Clark tried to coo the baby quiet but the infant was having none of it.

'So he had what? Information? Connections? A new job?' Jenny tried to concentrate, to filter out the baby and dog in the background.

'I don't know. It sounded suspicious. That's all I know. Please find him Constable. He's all I've got. Our parents are gone. My husband is a dropkick.' The woman sniffed.

'I understand. I'll do everything I can to find him but if you think of anything more specific, please let me know.' The vision of someone setting Ms Clark's house on fire and the baby burning alive filled her mind.

'Ms Clark. I don't know exactly what Curtis has gotten into, but you need to find yourself somewhere else to stay. Do you have a friend maybe?'

'I told you, it's only Curtis and me.'

Jenny collected her thoughts. 'You need to find a friend, a motel, maybe even your ex if he's not abusive.'

'What is going on?' Her voice quivered close to tears now. The poor woman. A newborn, a missing brother and now she needed to find a safe place to stay.

'I don't know for sure Ms Clark, but I'm investigating a murder here in Coober Pedy and if Curtis's get rich scheme has anything to do with the woman's death, well... Let's just say if they know Curtis, they might know you.'

The woman whimpered. The last thing Jenny wanted to do was scare her, but she knew first-hand how dangerous this arsonist was. 'Ms Clark, I'll have someone from your local police department call in. I'm sure they can find somewhere for you to stay.'

'But I've just had a baby and I don't know anything.' Her voiced rose an octave, then fell away to a hushed whisper.

'I'm calling someone now. Collect up your supplies for the baby and pack a bag for yourself. Okay?'

There was a moment of silence as the woman drew a shuddering breath, sniffed to clear her nose and answered. 'Okay.'

Chapter 29

'I have to head back later today. My job's done. The BnS crime-scene, the truck, the body. I've gathered all the evidence I can. I need to run more substance tests on the truck and confirm the accelerant.'

'Thanks for your help McGregor.' Sergeant Mackenzie sat behind his desk, his laptop closed in front of him. 'Let us know if anything new crops up.'

'I will.'

'She likely knew her attacker well enough to get cornered by them.' Jenny said.

'Or they were big enough to forcibly restrain her.' Philips spoke from the doorway, keeping watch on the front desk.

Jenny scribbled on the whiteboard, next to the photo of Curtis. 'Curtis's sister phoned me just as I was leaving last night. He isn't with her, but what she told me confirms our theory of blackmail.'

'Why do you say that?' Sergeant Mackenzie sat back, his fingers intertwined in front of his chest.

'She said he promised to bring her money, enough she didn't have to worry about bringing up her baby alone.'

'Did she know what he had?' O'Connell folded his arms as he sat on the corner of Sarge's desk, his eyes on hers.

'Unfortunately, no.'

'Blackmail.' O'Connell chewed his lip 'Balsy for a guy in his mid-twenties.'

'I'm thinking Melinda and Rachel came out here to keep Rachel safe. I think they found something while Rachel was working with Hayes. Maybe Curtis and Rachel got close then. Maybe they already knew each other from Melinda and Jake's history? Either way, I think he convinced Rachel to use whatever she knows for blackmail instead of bringing it to the police.'

'Maybe that's why Rachel was asking for Nigel Smart? Maybe she now wants to hand the information off to him? If Curtis is involved in blackmail, and Rachel found some sort of evidence… McGregor.' Penny turned to Sarge.

'Yes Sir?'

'Have you packed up your evidence yet?'

'Some of it Sir. But not all. What do you need?'

'I think you need to go over the Mercedes' contents more thoroughly.'

'I'll follow that up now.'

'Let's go people. Find that evidence. Find a murderer.' Sergeant Mackenzie flicked his hands in a backwards wave to send the team on their way.

Jenny whispered over Penny's shoulder. 'Looks like you can't get away that easily.'

Penny grinned. 'Time for drinks tonight then. Sorry you missed Nick the other night. Have you spoken with him?

'No, I've been so busy. I have a photo I'd love you to check for me though.'

'Sure, what is it?'

'It's Nick's dad's suicide scene. You're more experienced than me. Maybe you can spot something obvious but something doesn't look quite right.'

'Happy to try. Let's grab a beer after work and I'll go over it then.'

Philips collected his utility vest from his locker and grabbed the keys. 'Ready to canvas the neighbourhood for any sign of Newman?'

'Let's go.' Jenny pressed her fingers to her temples, closed her eyes, then rubbed them. Her head ached. 'First I need coffee. Badly!'

Chapter 30

'Okay!' Penny entered, two evidence boxes piled high held closely to her chest. 'Can someone help me unload all these boxes?' She peered around the boxes, trying to make sure she didn't knock into anything on the way in.

'I've got it.' O'Connell pushed to his feet and rushed to lift the countertop open for Penny to come through. 'You need to chase up Newman's army records.' He waggled his finger at her impatiently.

'Yes Sir.' She fought the urge to salute. O'Connell was usually the calm voice of reason. He must have been as frustrated with the lag in this case as she was.

'Oh, what's up?' Penny put the boxes on the counter and scanned Jenny's face, one eyebrow raised. Jenny nearly laughed at the comical expression.

'Come on McGregor. You can gossip later. Williams has work to do.'

'But I'm just helping with the case.' Penny picked up the boxes and pouted.

'That way!' The Senior Constable pointed aggressively to Penny's makeshift lab before hurrying outside to empty the car. Penny rolled her eyes, her lip rose in unison with her eyebrow. Jenny giggled.

The tall, broad-shouldered scientist wasn't used to being bossed around. She worked autonomously, on site, away from even her own authorities. Forensic teams were lead at any scene they attended. Even detectives did as they were told around Penny.

'Okay. I'll go through the boxes and focus on finding anything that could contain blackmailing info.' Penny rushed past with another load of boxes, O'Connell right behind her.

'Sir, can we get that warrant for Curtis and Rachel's phone records issued yet? And maybe Newman's.'

'I don't think so. We've got no proof Curtis is blackmailing anyone yet. Only that he expected to come into money. Any luck canvassing for Newman?'

'Nothing Sir. No one has seen the guy. Has anyone confirmed Hayes was on the plane?'

'She's off-limits Williams.'

'There is no harm in checking, surely. If she was on it, no issue. If she wasn't, then maybe we can speak to Roberts' superiors and get some joy. We've already requested the footage.'

'I'll see what I can do. I'll contact the airport in town again.' O'Connell tapped the top of the boxes. 'Take these to McGregor and sift through the evidence while I try and get a warrant and chase up the service records.'

'Yes Sir'

Jenny lifted the boxes and followed Penny down the hallway.

Penny was busy spreading out the contents of the Mercedes over every surface of the breakroom. It was an ideal temporary lab, with a kitchen, loads of bench space and a large table occupying the centre of the room.

Strewn on the table were two suitcases, a backpack, a laptop, picnic hamper and various folders of paperwork. Piled high on the side bench were personal hygiene products and a velvet and chrome makeup case larger than a camera bag.

Jenny wondered how Rachel was getting on with all her personal belongings in police custody. Everything they travelled to Coober Pedy with, was laid out as evidence in Melinda's murder investigation.

'How's it going?' Jenny stepped forward, scratching her head, wondering where to start. 'Where do you want me?'

Penny remained focussed on fingerprinting Melinda's bright pink hard-shell suitcase but one hand rose and pointed to a stack of Manilla folders on the table.

'Grab some gloves and try that lot there.' She waved her hand, then went back to placing clear tape over a series of black prints. 'I was going to do this back in Adelaide, but…'

'Find something?' Jenny flicked on a pair of surgical gloves before picking up a folder.

'Not sure yet, but I never ran the contents of the Mercedes for fingerprints. It wasn't the crime scene, but there are at least two sets of prints here I can't account for from the victim or her friend Rachel.'

'Someone else already went through the Mercedes before we got there?'

'Possibly.'

'Newman's maybe. His prints will be on file, so maybe run them as quick as you can.'

Penny's head snapped around, a wicked grin teased at the corner of her mouth. 'Excellent. I'm on it now.' She pressed the clear tape to a piece of white card, placed it alongside two others on the table and snapped a series of photos.

Disappearing without a word, she left Jenny to consider the file in her hand. There were no logos, nothing on the file tab to indicate what it was or where it came from. Jenny opened the folder and sighed. Empty space greeted her. Whatever was inside, was long gone.

Fighting frustration, she continued her search through the contents on the table, stopping at a red satin clutch. She picked it up, rolled it over in her hand, then put it back down, turning to follow Penny.

She found the scientist sitting at the desk. 'You got Newman's details?'

'Yep, and I've checked his prints, one set are his, and I think the other set are a woman's.'

'Do we have Hayes's prints?'

'No. She's squeaky clean.'

'Of course she is.'

'Sir.' O'Connell turned from the filing cabinet. 'We found files in the car's contents, but they were empty. No logo or anything to identify where they came from ether. But while I was looking at a red purse out the back, I remembered the purple purse and how someone brazenly stole it from the crime scene Friday night. I'm thinking there was something in it, but if they got what they wanted, they probably wouldn't still be hunting Rachel and Curtis because they'd have nothing to use as blackmail.

'Possibly, but what she knows is still in her head, or she might have a copy. Or maybe they convinced whoever they are blackmailing they have other proof.'

'That's the point Sir. I don't think whoever took the purse got what they wanted.'

'You think Rachel still has it?'

'Or it's still in the purse. Can I take another go over it?'

'That's McGregor's call. It's in her custody.'

Penny gazed up at the mention of her name. 'What's up?'

'Can we take another look at the purse or did you send it to Adelaide with the other evidence?'

'I still have it here. I brought it back in with the vehicle contents. It's the only real piece of evidence we found so far.'

'Excellent. Let's go over it again.'

'I'll meet you in the lab.'

'Before you two go anywhere,' Jenny turned at the tone of Sergeant Mackenzie's voice. 'I've just heard back from the airport. They've finally sent the security footage over Philips requested.'

'Let's do it.' Jenny grinned. The Boss didn't like ruffling feathers and the fact he'd chased down evidence on Hayes when Roberts warned them off surprised her.

'Don't get your hopes up.' Sarge pointed to the computer on O'Connell's desk. 'It should be on the email by now. Take a look.'

Penny slid out of the seat at O'Connell's desk as Jenny clicked keys before bothering to sit down. Her whole body tingled from the inside out. In her mind, Hayes was the lynchpin in this whole investigation.

Finding the email, Jenny clicked on the attachment. The time and date stamp showed Friday at 10.05 a.m.. 'This is it.' She hit play as everyone hovered over the one, small computer screen like it was a shrine.

'Do we have grounds to get some of those search warrants now?' She peered up at her boss.

Chapter 31

Jenny waited, but no one answered her. She'd never seen O'Connell or the Sergeant speechless.

'We have Newman's prints on Melinda's suitcase,' Penny prompted. 'And an unknown woman's.'

'My orders from Roberts' department were clear. We are not to move against Hayes.'

'But Sir. She never got on her flight. She could have been in town a week before Melinda was killed. She could have been hunting Rachel. Maybe she still is.' Jenny fidgeted in her seat.

'Slow down Williams. I get you're excited about being right.' O'Connell grinned, his hand holding firm on top of her shoulder. 'But we need to get all our ducks in a row before we make accusations against Hayes.'

'I'll get a warrant for Newman's phone and credit-card records. We still don't have enough for Curtis and Rachel's.' Sergeant Mackenzie stepped toward his office, stopping, he turned back. 'Keep digging Williams. We're getting there.'

'Come on, let's check out this purse.' Penny dragged Jenny from the desk, toward her lab.

'Okay.' Jenny let herself be led away reluctantly. Procedure sucked at times. Roberts was protecting a possible murderer. The legal system of warrants and due cause could be putting Rachel and Curtis's life on the line.

Penny handed Jenny a fresh pair of gloves. 'I went over this pretty thoroughly.' Retrieving the purse from a paper evidence bag, she noted the time and date on the evidence log. 'I'll be really pissed if I missed something. Whoever took the purse likely found what they were looking for.'

'Maybe. Maybe not. If it's still there and you missed it, I have no doubt it's well hidden.' Jenny pulled on the gloves before running her fingers over the outside of the silky patterned bag. 'You swabbed it, did the usual forensic thing, but you weren't looking for a hidden storage device. It could be in the lining. I can't see Rachel keeping paper copies.'

'True,' Penny pulled out a gadget from her forensic kit 'but there's any easier way to find a memory card.' She turned on the machine, picked up the purse from under Jenny's fingers and passed the device over the bag. It buzzed and crackled as it travelled over the metal clasp. Penny adjusted a setting and passed over the clasp again. The buzzing intensified.

'What is it?'

'It's a metal detector, but I've set it to gold.' Penny put the gadget down and studied the clasp. Unsatisfied, she placed the purse down on the table, fished in her bag to produce a pair of magnifying glasses before putting them on to take another look.

'Talk – about – spy – tech.'

'What?' Jenny hunched down closer, studying what Penny found.

'This clasp opens up like a locket.' She reached into her bag, retrieved a pair of long-nosed tweezers and poked around inside the ornate clasp. Two attempts later, it clicked open to reveal a micro-SD card, which Penny pulled out. 'I think this might be what you've been looking for.'

Chapter 32

Jenny fidgeted while the card was checked for prints. Satisfied, Penny loaded the micro-SD card into an adapter and pushed it into her laptop card slot. Jenny stepped up to hover over her shoulder. A single folder popped up on the computer. They held their breath as Penny clicked it open.

A page of photos displayed in tiny icons too small to see clearly. Penny clicked a few keys and the icons became larger.

'Open that one.' Jenny pointed to the top right-hand corner, her heart racing, her fingers shaking. She fought for calm as the file came up. 'These appear to be legitimate adoption records. They must be dodgy or Rachel wouldn't have gone to the trouble of hiding them. This is what Curtis must have been talking about on the video with Roberts. He's letting Hayes get away with this.'

'Bastard.' Penny growled.

'I need to tell Sarge.'

'He's already told you the detective and Hayes are off limits.'

'Yes, but we've got evidence now that Hayes is doing something illegal. Now we might be able to convince Roberts' superiors to get a warrant for Hayes's phone and credit-card records.'

Penny shrugged; her expression lacked Jenny's conviction.

'Do you think you might be a bit fixated on Roberts? He's got a job to do, just like us.'

'Maybe he's spent too long undercover, but something doesn't feel right about him. Don't you think?'

'He's an undercover cop. They live in a different world. They take on another persona entirely. Live, eat and breathe it, or die.'

'But he told Curtis to stay out of his way. He could be our killer.'

'He could have just been trying to make sure the guy didn't get killed, like Melinda. Do you really believe he's the murderer?'

Jenny sighed. 'Nooo! But he annoys me.' Penny laughed. 'Besides, he's protecting Hayes and Hayes knows Newman. This is all linked.' She pointed to the photo in front of her. 'I need to go through these images. If this is what got Melinda killed and made Rachel a target, then I'll hopefully find what I'm looking for there.'

'Well I think I'm done now. I'll take my evidence back to Adelaide and work from there.'

'Oh damn!' Jenny pouted. 'I'll miss you. It's been awesome having you here.'

Penny shimmied out of her chair. Jenny stepped back to give her room. 'I'm not gone yet. I think I can manage another drink tonight before I head off in the morning.' 'Sounds like a plan. In the meantime, I have phone records to hunt down.'

'You can't cover everything. Where's Philips?'

'He'll be back soon. I think Tommy is sick and he and Dianna have taken him to the hospital to get him checked.'

'He's a cute kid. Hope it's nothing serious.' Penny placed items into an evidence box, carefully checking labels and ticking the evidence log.

'He'll be fine. Danny said he gets asthma. A dose of Ventolin on the nebuliser and he'll be all good, but you can't be too careful with asthma. Jenny retrieved the micro-SD card from Penny's computer. 'I've gotta run. See you tonight.'

Jenny vaguely heard Penny respond as she scooted down the hall to the main office area. O'Connell sat behind his computer, a smile on his face. 'Sarge managed to get Curtis's phone records, based on the video.'

'That's awesome. Any luck on Hayes' or Newman's?'

O'Connell shook his head. 'Nope, but we'll keep working on it.'

She stepped toward the desk. 'Anything interesting in Curtis's records?'

'His mobile hasn't been used for a few days, but the last call he made was to the William Creek Pub.'

Her adrenalin spiked. 'I'll call Mrs B.. They've got those units out there.'

'They have.' O'Connell grinned.

'Sir.' She attempted to stay calm and slow down. 'Penny and I just uncovered a memory card in the purple purse.' O'Connell's smile disappeared. 'It's got photos of adoption records, with the legal firm's logo on them, but they must be bogus.'

'Worth blackmailing for?'

'I've got the files here.' Jenny held the card aloft. 'Let's find out.'

'Hand it over.' O'Connell held his hand out for the card. 'I'll print a few of these out for our files.' The laser printer started up on the other side of the room. The humming became whirring as the first file started to print.

Jenny retrieved it and waited for the rest. Her eyes wandered over the information, trying to see if there was anything to indicate it was illegal, not a regular adoption document.

She reached down to collect the last printout, her eyes fixed on the copy in her hand. She sucked in a breath. Her skin tingled with excitement. This was what they needed. Finally, a break in the case.

'What is it?' O'Connell's eyes locked on hers.

Jenny rushed over to him, still reading, still trying to take it all in.

'Let me check it isn't a coincidence.' She shuffled the papers to bring another file to the surface. 'No, it's not.' She hurried around to O'Connell's side of the desk, slammed the pile down and pointed to what she found. 'Each of these is for a non-Australian adoption. An Afghan infant to be exact.'

'Michael Newman contracted over there.'

'Yes, ex-army, currently a fire and safety officer. It all fits. But we still don't have his service records.'

'Look who signed off on each infant.' O'Connell pointed to the signature at the bottom of the page.

'These are all Hayes's files.'

'Makes sense. If Rachel or Melinda copied them.'

'Surely she would know she was brokering illegal adoption, not legal ones.'

'I think she knows. Check out this signature here.' O'Connell laid out three of the files side by side.

'They are all the same? All three of these, what? Six-month-old infants can't come from the same mother.'

'Who's bringing in these infants?'

'Michael Newman maybe. When was the last one processed?'

O'Connell studied the unprinted files on his computer, opening each one and checking dates. 'The last one was dated less than three months ago.

'Is illegal adoption a good enough reason to kill someone?' Jenny studied the screen full of dozens of records.

'It is when the buyers are from the top one hundred richest business owners in the country.' O'Connell zoomed in on one of the adoptees. Jenny whistled. The guy was heir to a media mega house. His father owned the most influential, politically affiliated newspaper in the country.

'No wonder you never see photos of his kid.'

'Well when you own the paper, you can cut any story you want. They must have paid a fortune to get a baby. With a price tag like these guys would pay, it's no wonder Newman wanted to kill Rachel to shut her up.'

'Now I understand why they disappeared.'

'Exactly, but what made Curtis think he could blackmail Hayes or Newman when families like this were buying babies illegally? These people have clout, lots of it.' O'Connell shook his head slowly. 'We'll be lucky if Curtis and Rachel aren't already dead.'

Chapter 33

Jenny returned to the front counter as Philips entered. His cheeks were flushed, but the smile on his face told her Tommy was going to be alright.

'Hey. How's Tommy?'

'Good now. Dianna has him back home.'

'You look fried, but that's fantastic news.'

Philips scanned the station. 'Where are we at?'

'I could say you didn't miss much, but you did,' she smiled teasingly. 'We found a micro-SD card in the clasp of the purple purse.'

'Really!' Philips rushed around the counter, slamming the pass-through accidentally. Jenny jumped. He winced.

'Yep. Whoever took it from the crime scene didn't know where the information was hidden.'

'What did it have on it?'

She handed him one of the printed files. 'Illegal adoption records, well, they are made to look legal, but put together, side by side, it's obvious the mother on each one is the same person and they are Afghan babies.'

'Newman!'

'That was my first thought. I'm still trying to chase down information on where he served and when. The military files aren't easily accessible. O'Connell has managed to get a warrant, but they are taking their sweet time.'

'What about phone and credit-cards?'

'Requested. They should be in later today or Monday, but we did get a hit with Curtis's phone records. His last call was the William Creek Pub. I was just about to follow up with Mrs B. now.'

'I can do that if you like?'

'Actually, can you chase down where Roberts has been? I need to ask him what he knows about Curtis blackmailing Hayes and Newman. We need to convince him to let us at her.'

'I could have asked him before.' Philips pursed his lips and frowned.

'What do you mean?' Jenny stared at him.

'He was at the hospital.' Philips pointed over his shoulder in totally the wrong direction, 'Nearly bumped into him in the triage.'

'Is he still there?' Jenny shifted from one foot to the other impatiently.

'No idea.' Philips shrugged casually.

'Okay. You call Mrs B. and find out if Curtis is staying there. I'm heading over to the hospital now. Is Nev on duty?'

'He was. Why?'

'Because I can get him to play delay tactics.'

'Good luck with that.' Philips scoffed as Jenny jogged out the office.

Pulling her phone from her pocket, she dialled, then waited while rummaging in her other pocket for her keys. With her uniform on, she wasn't going to be able to go unnoticed, but at least her rusty car wouldn't attract too much attention as she drove up. Roberts was an undercover cop. The last thing he needed was a cop car rocking up at the hospital.

'Nev. You got a tattooed bikie guy in there still?'

'Ah, yeah.' The hesitation in his voice told her he was probably standing near Roberts. 'Don't say anything, but find an excuse to keep him there another ten minutes.'

'Sure. You can bring him straight in to Emergency.' Nev was trying to sound casual.

'Good, thanks. He's not dangerous, so don't panic.' She wanted to keep Nev from giving away too much. Roberts was a detective, so reading people and weird body language was second nature. 'Tell him I'm your girlfriend, bringing my dad in or something.'

'It's okay. I'm on duty anyway. I'll look after your dad hun, but I've got to go. Okay?'

'Thanks Nev.' Jenny dropped the phone on the passenger seat, turned the key and backed out of the parking area, trying not to kick up gravel as she planted her foot.

Pulling up outside Emergency, her stomach knotted. Speaking with Roberts was important, but she didn't want to blow his cover. They were supposed to be on the same side, even if his job meant protecting a possible murderer.

A wave of cool air swamped her as she rushed through the double doors into the Emergency waiting room. Unfamiliar with this part of the hospital, she stopped to orientate herself.

A nurse sat behind a Perspex window, a line of three people before her. Jenny was thankful for her uniform as the nurse didn't blink when she strolled past the desk and through the double doors leading to the triage area.

The smell of bleach and disinfectant grew stronger as she approached. Three cubicles with blue curtains lined each side of the room. The first two on either side were open, and empty. The last one on the right was closed. Jenny could hear Nev's voice.

'I think you could do with a tetanus shot, but if you are refusing, it's up to you. I'll need you to sign this waiver though.'

'I need to get out of here. Now.' The sound of boots hitting faux white-marble lino made her speed up.

'What's the rush?' Jenny pushed the curtain aside, stepped in, drawing it closed for Roberts' protection.

'How's your dear old dad then Hun?' Roberts sneered.

'He's good. Last time we spoke.' Jenny didn't miss a beat, but she was surprised Roberts picked up on the ruse. 'How'd you know?'

'I saw his caller ID as he answered.'

'You know my mobile number.' She faked an eyelash flutter. 'I'm flattered.' *How did he have her number?*

'Don't be.'

Nev watched the exchange, relaxing as the banter continued. 'You know each other.'

'Don't say that too loudly.' Roberts put his finger over his lips conspiratorially.

Nev tapped his nose and backed out of the cubical slowly. 'Sorry. I'll leave you to it then.'

Jenny's legs were splayed, her arms crossed, her expression firm. 'I need to interview Hayes.'

'You can't.' Roberts shook his head emphatically. 'I've already told you to leave her alone.' He crossed his arms.

'Why? You two an item or something?' Roberts rolled his eyes, but he dropped his arms. Jenny wasn't giving up. 'She's the key to our murder investigation.' She kept her voice low, stepping in close alongside the detective, shooing him over with her hand so she could sit next to him on the narrow hospital bed.

'She has critical information I need for my investigation and in typical lawyer speak, told me to keep you off her back or she'd disappear along with my case.'

'And that didn't set off alarm bells!' Jenny waited, her finger tapping on her knee. Roberts said nothing. 'What's this is all about then?' Jenny pointed to Roberts' bandaged arm, wishing she arrived in time to see the wound before it was covered.

'Nothing. It's a Harlequin thing.'

'Really? You upset someone in the gang? I didn't think any of them were here. It being not a Harlequin drug area and all.'

'Nature of the business. Let's just say the gang weren't exactly happy when their meth lab blew up.' He shrugged, but something in his eyes told her there was more to the injury than his gang related work.

'What! You told my sergeant that the Harlequins didn't have a drug lab…' He shushed her with his finger. 'Never mind, I don't care about drugs. I want to catch a murderer,' she sighed.

'And I'm trying to get some high-ranking Harlequins off the street.'

'By getting Curtis and Rachel killed?' Jenny studied the detective. 'You told Curtis to back off at the BnS didn't you?'

'I told him that blackmail could get him killed.' Roberts' shoulders slumped.

'You knew he was blackmailing Hayes.'

'Of course I did. Hayes is knee-deep in Harlequin crap and I'm using her to get what I want. She told me what Curtis was up to. I told her I'd get him to back off and retrieve the evidence he had.'

'But he didn't.'

'He didn't.' Roberts sniffed, his nostrils flared.

'And now Melinda is dead and he and Rachel are missing, trying to stay alive. Hayes knows Newman is trying to kill them. She could have been involved in killing Melinda for all you know.'

Roberts' eyes darted to hers. For an undercover cop, he wasn't great at hiding his emotions. He hadn't expected her to know about Newman. Or did he? As an undercover cop, he should be an expert at playing someone he wasn't. It could easily be a ploy, a persona put on for her benefit.

'Hayes isn't a murderer, but even if she is, the Harlequins are in another league. Prostitution. Drugs. Murder for hire. Whatever she and Newman are into, isn't anything compared to what I can do busting the Harlequins wide open.'

'You put the top dogs of the Harlequins in jail and another guy steps up to the plate. Or worse, another gang does. Just legalise the stuff, regulate it, charge bloody tax on the income and use it to deal with addiction. Then you can do some real policing, like solving murders and protecting innocent families from having their kids stolen.'

'That's easy to say, but the problem isn't that simple. Drugs are only a small piece of this pie. The Harlequins are deep into government, big business. They don't only make their money from the illegal drug trade. They make a fortune from paid hits, extortion and stuff that would probably give you nightmares.

'All I can do is deal with the murder I've got now. Your trade-off doesn't sit well with me. Sacrificing one life for possibly many more later isn't okay. Deep down you know that, don't you?'

Roberts shook his head and pushed off the bed. 'I'm leaving. You need to find Curtis and Rachel and work this out without Hayes. That's not only what I say, it's what my superiors are telling you, so make it happen Williams. I've seen your stats. You'll figure it out.'

Roberts brushed the curtain aside, then stopped as Jenny spoke. 'But will I do it before someone else dies?'

He turned back. 'That's your job. You do yours, I'll do mine.' He disappeared behind the blue fabric, leaving Jenny sitting on the bed, staring at the vacant space.

Chapter 34

The condensation rolled down the beer glass, soaking the cardboard coaster. She ran her finger around the rim, her mind wandering as the conversation around her sounded muffled.

'Hey. It's my last night. Put work stuff out of your head girl.' Penny grinned cheekily, an infectious smile Jenny couldn't help but return.

'Sorry. I'm just worried.'

'You can't save people from their own stupidity Jenny. Curtis and Rachel know you're here to help.'

'Yeah, but they probably don't trust anyone after what happened to Melinda.'

'Maybe. But you called Curtis's sister. You told her if he called, to let him know you would take care of him if he came in. The rest is up to them.'

Philips slid into the seat next to her, beer jug in hand. 'Mrs B. said they've not turned up at the pub.'

'I'll still head out tomorrow and see if I can track them down. We've canvassed all over town with no joy.'

Jenny called every real estate agent and accommodation place in Coober Pedy. No one matching Curtis' or Rachel's description was staying with them. The fact they had no idea where Hayes and Newman were holed up bothered her nearly as much.

Roberts must have hidden her, or maybe he sent her home? Either way, there was no sign of her or Michael Newman, but the outback was vast. They could be hiding out at a farm-stay, a bed and breakfast or even camping out, although Hayes didn't strike her as the slumming it out in the bush type.

'You want some company?' Nev put a load of frosty beer glasses on the table. 'I'm off shift tomorrow.'

'Thanks for the offer but I'll be catching up with Nick if I can.'

'And three's a crowd.'

'Not at all.' She couldn't explain in front of Philips. She hoped to spend a few days digging into Nick's father's death and seeing if there was anything else hiding in the cellar below the William Creek Station homestead.

'I'm helping Nick with his dad's death.' At least she could be open about that. She wondered if her boss got anywhere with Kent Murphy?

'Yeah. I heard about it. Nasty business.' Nev flipped the menu over on the table as he spoke. Jenny's stomach grumbled.

'Nick doesn't believe his father committed suicide.' Jenny sipped her beer, relaxing into the atmosphere. The motel bar and restaurant was noisy. Cheryl and Stan were busy serving at the bar, running from one end to the other to keep up with the growing crowd.

'A shame they never did an autopsy.' Penny sipped her white wine. 'Don't forget to show me that photo.'

'I have it on my phone. Glad you reminded me. This current case has me preoccupied. I don't know where my brain is.' She pulled her phone from her pocket, scrolling through pictures, she found the one of Nick's dad… lying face down on the kitchen table, gun in hand.

'Good to see you're not infallible.' Philips grinned, swigged his beer then wiped the froth from his top lip.

Jenny handed the phone to Penny, 'Ha ha.'

Penny zoomed in with her fingers, squinted, pursed her lips and jumped as the phone buzzed with an incoming call.

Handing it back, Jenny recognised the caller ID, stood and excused herself from the table with a wave of one finger. 'Give me a sec.'

She scuttled toward the beer garden, hoping to get better reception. The crackling line told her she didn't manage it.

'Constable?'

'Yes Mrs B. I'm here. Give me a second. I need to go outside to get a better signal.' She rushed further into the courtyard. 'Can you hear me?'

'Yes luv. Got you now. Sorry to jump straight to it, but this place is hectic tonight.' Jenny could hear shouts and hoots in the background. 'Got a few Sydney-siders flying in for the weekend. The couple you put the feelers out for. They checked in a few minutes ago.'

'I'll be there in a few hours Mrs B. Let the station know if they leave. Do you have a registration number?'

'Of course I do luv. It's a requirement of any booking. I'll text it to you.'

'You're a gem. I'll see you soon.'

Jenny shoved her phone back in her pocket, resisting the urge to run back into the bar. She needed to report in to her boss before she went off on a tangent. Her last few cases were solved but could have ended badly. This time, she was under strict orders to keep everyone in the loop.

'Philips. Our lost couple have been found.' She tapped him on the shoulder as she flew past, eyeing off her beer, knowing it was going to have to wait now.

'I'll say goodbye now then.' Penny rose, put her glass down and stepped closer to Jenny, giving her a sisterly hug. 'You be careful.'

'I'm always careful.' Penny wasn't the only one to laugh out loud.

'What?'

'Come on Williams. Let's go.' Philips left his half-finished beer reluctantly. 'I'll drive.'

'You sure?'

'I'm sure.' Philips led the way from the restaurant.

'You call it in while I grab our gear from the station.'

She retrieved her phone, backpack and followed Philips out the double glass doors. He pressed the unlock on the police Landcruiser as they reached the front of the station across the road from the motel.

'Can you check the email or fax while you are there? I've been waiting on Newman's army records. We need to know who might be chasing Rachel and Curtis.'

'Will do.'

Philips disappeared into the station as Jenny dialled Sergeant Mackenzie's mobile. The call rang out. Switching to O'Connell's private mobile, she dialled and waited.

'What's up Williams?'

'Sorry to bother you Sir. Mrs B. just notified me that Rachel and Curtis have turned up at the Pub. Philips and I will head out to see if we can bring them in for questioning.'

'Alright. I'll come down the station and man the radio. You and Philips keep in touch. Got it?'

'Yes Sir. I tried Sarge, but didn't get an answer.'

'All good Williams. I'll let him know.'

'Thanks Sir.' She hung up. The hair on the back of her neck stood to attention. Peering into the shadows, she waited, the sound of her own breathing was the only thing she heard.

A noise made her turn to see Philips locking the station door. A tingle down her spine told her someone was watching them as they got into the Landcruiser.

'Here. This was on the fax machine.' Philips handed Jenny two pieces of paper. She turned on the interior light as Philips started the engine.

A black and white photo occupied the left-hand corner. The top of the page read Corporal Michael James Newman.

Scanning quickly, she noted his dishonourable discharge after serving in Afghanistan. There was no further explanation, but she didn't need one.

The guy was a lethal weapon, and according to his army record, couldn't be trusted. 'He's been discharged, dishonourably.'

'Hayes got him off those arson charges too.'

'Maybe the army knew he was smuggling infants out of Afghanistan?'

'What's his training?'

'Weapons of course.' She scanned the file, using her phone as a torch. 'Damn!'

'What?'

'He's not only a fire safety officer. As we feared, he's an explosives expert.'

'So he's got the skillset needed to blow up a truck.'

'It was a diesel fire. Almost anyone could have lit it up. But fire is this guy's weapon of choice.'

'Too neat maybe?' Philips glanced at her as she put her phone away.

'If it quacks like a duck, it's probably a duck.' Jenny put the papers into her backpack and placed it at her feet. Reaching for her utility vest, she put it on and patted it, reassuringly.

'That's very profound.'

'I thought so.' Jenny gazed out the windscreen as the sun disappeared over the horizon. Her stomach rolled and pitched. The sensation of being watched hadn't abated.

Where was Newman? On paper, he looked good for Melinda's murder and the truck fire, but was Philips right? Was the package too neatly wrapped?

Chapter 35

Jenny texted O'Connell and Mackenzie as they drove from the outskirts of Coober Pedy. *Let us know if you get anything back on Newman's cards or phone.* She hit send and dropped her mobile into the pocket of her utility vest.

With a two-hour drive ahead of them, Jenny needed a distraction from the investigation or anxiety might get the better of her.

'How's Tommy doing?'

Philips glanced at her sideways, his features softened. Being country cops meant their work and family lives were often intertwined.

'He's doing much better. Dianna was pretty worried about him. He's always been a little bit sickly. If he catches a cold, it almost always ends in a hospital visit.'

'My middle brother Ben was a bit like that.'

'I didn't know you had brothers.'

'Yeah. Three. I'm the youngest and the only girl.'

'That explains a lot,' he chuckled.

'I get that a lot.'

'You don't talk much about your family.'

Guilt niggled at her conscience, but now wasn't the time to bring her family history up.

She shrugged. 'We're close, but we don't do the whole phone every week thing. I guess it comes from our farming background but we are all very independent, so we get on with life and catch up for special functions, occasionally.'

'What's with Nick's dad?'

'It's a long story.' Jenny didn't want to get into it. If she did, it might give away her reasons for moving to the desert outback town.

'We've got nearly two hours.'

There was a long silence as she wrestled with how much she could tell her partner.

'Nick's initial reaction to me was cold. Harsh even. I wondered about it. After a few meetings with him, I discovered his dad died... apparently suicide and he didn't trust the cops because he didn't believe it was suicide.'

'Before my time. I only vaguely knew about it.'

'Holmes caught the case.'

'And you think he missed something?'

'I think he was busy.' She didn't want to open that can of worms again.

'What have you found?'

'Like Penny said, no autopsy was done. The body was prepared for burial by the time Nick got back from university. His mother went missing at the same time.'

'So if Nick doesn't believe his dad committed suicide and his mum went missing at the same time. Does he think she might have done it?'

'Not seriously. There's got to be something else behind it.'

'You said it yourself, if it quacks like a duck....' He didn't finish the statement. Police training told them the most obvious answer was usually the right one, but she was sure it wasn't in Nick's case. Maybe whoever was involved in her aunt and cousin's disappearance was involved with Nick's mum going missing too?

'It could be nothing. But I promised him I'd follow it up and Sarge is considering reopening the investigation.'

'You two an item?'

She squirmed in her seat. 'No.' She needed to change the subject. Before it got awkward. 'I spoke with Roberts at the hospital.'

He smiled knowingly.

'He's protecting Hayes as part of a deal.'

'Why can't he get the information we need out of her and still keep her out of it?'

'Bit hard if she's guilty.' Philips nodded understanding. 'She told him to get us off her case or she'd disappear.'

She studied the side mirror as red dust floated in their wake. The effect of the red haze against the setting sun appeared like a firestorm on the horizon. Philips hit the brakes. Jenny lunged into her seatbelt as a huge kangaroo bounced out in front of the headlights. It was gone in a heartbeat.

They chatted about the case, the history of Coober Pedy and how Danny met his wife until the lights of the William Creek Pub came into view.

Parked to the left of the pub was the vehicle Rachel and Curtis were driving. Jenny recalled the registration number from memory. Philips drew the Landcruiser up alongside. Stepping out, she strapped on her pistol belt and checked her utility vest.

Still in civilian clothing from the restaurant, she pulled her police hat on to help identify her. It gave her a sense of security, which puzzled her a moment. Joining the police force was her only goal after Melanie went missing, but now she wore the uniform every day – it was a part of her.

Circling the older model Ford Maverick, she stopped to peer in the windows. A few take away packets was all she could see.

'No one's in there.' Turning on her heel she joined Philips as he stepped onto the dirt pathway leading along the veranda in front of the pub.

An explosion shook the whole building, sending debris raining down over the tin veranda roof onto the dust below. Adrenalin hit Jenny's system, as shouts came from all directions.

Disorientated, she scanned the immediate area as people spilled out of the old timber and ironclad pub. The smell of smoke filled the air. Screams erupted from behind the pub.

Calls for water, help, police and C.F.S. made Jenny look at Philips. Their legs were moving before they thought about it.

Rounding the corner together, they stopped. Jenny hesitated a split second before realising the block of tired clad accommodation units was alight. People ran in all directions as Mrs B.'s daughter Rebecca and son Mick reeled out a fire hose with practised precision.

'Anyone inside?' Jenny called as she grabbed the hose and helped.

'Yes!' Mrs B. ran up behind them. 'That's where the couple is!'

'Damn!' Jenny let go of the hose and bolted full speed for the front door. Her heart pounded. She put her hand up over her head against the heat.

'Williams!' Philips' voice sounded hollow, distant against the pulse banging inside her ears. 'Jenny. No!'

Chapter 36

Water drizzled over her head, quickly turning into a torrent as the fire pump kicked up to full power. Touching the door handle with the back of her hand, she snatched it away. Water poured over the rim of her Akubra, making it difficult to see.

Lifting it off, she tossed it to the side and ran to the rear of the building. The sound of muffled voices made her shiver. A thump on a small rear window caught her off-guard. She jumped instinctively, but turned to the source to see a tormented face plastered against the tiny glass pane.

Jenny couldn't make out what Rachel was saying, but the whites of her eyes were visible as her lips moved and her face contorted. Another thump on the glass, this time with less effort. She was fading fast, but the window opening was too small for her to pass through.

Jenny turned and rushed around the building, her lungs hurt, her legs pumped. She yelled as loud as she could. 'Phillips, get the car and a tow rope!'

She didn't wait to see if her partner heard her. Instead, she returned to the window, collected a large limestone rock and peered through the window. Rachel's face no longer stared out at her.

Standing back, she tossed the rock with as much effort as she could muster. It struck! Shattered glass spilled to the ground. Oxygen rushed in, feeding the fire. Not good, but if she didn't get fresh air in, Rachel would die of asphyxiation.

Smoke poured out as air filtered in.

Did they make it to the bathroom? She hoped so. Scurrying forward, Jenny pushed her face into the opening, hoping to see where they were. Instead, the thick smoke made her cough – her memory of nearly dying in a fire flooded back. She froze for a second, then shook herself.

'Rachel! Curtis! Hang on! Get away from the wall.' There was no reply, but it didn't matter. They were dead if she didn't get them out. The Landcruiser skidded to a halt outside the rear of the building.

Jenny tapped around the window frame with her knuckles as Philips jumped from the driver's side. 'Grab the rope.' She barked orders.

'I've got the winch.' Philips raced to the front bullbar and held up a hook attached to a thick wire cable in his left hand.

'You man the winch. I'll wrap this around the window frame.' She pulled her baton from her hip belt, smashing holes into the outside of the old fibro building, exposing timber frame and the windowsill.

Phillips disengaged the pin on the winch and rushed toward her with the cable. 'Be careful. That's probably Asbestos.'

'That's the least of their worries and if it is, that's good. It won't be burning down anytime soon.' She yelled over the beat of her own heart in her ears as water sprinkled down from the roof.

She wrapped the hook around and back on itself as Phillips rushed back to the winch button. Waving her hand, she indicated for him to take up the slack.

The winch whirred to life, the line began to grow taught. She focussed on the sound, blocking out the screams, the calls as people tried desperately to get the fire under control.

Another hose team arrived. Water sprinkled over her. The winch stopped. She stepped back, and snuck a glance at Philips. Her chest ached as she did a final assessment, then put her finger in the air, and spun it in a circle to give Philips the go ahead.

The winch motor kicked back in, the sound laboured for a few seconds, before the wall exploded – timbers jutted out in all direction as debris flew into the air. Jenny ignored it all as she ran forward before the debris hit the ground. Smoke billowed for a moment, then dissipated to reveal smashed tiles, broken framework and Rachel, fully clothed hunched down in the bathtub. Her eyes were open, wild and unfocussed.

Alongside her on what was left of the tiled floor was Curtis sprawled out and face down. 'Philips!' She screamed, but he was already at her side.

'You grab Curtis. I'll get Rachel out of here.'

Jenny turned back to Rachel, who was barely conscious. Struggling, she tried to pull the petite woman out of the tub, but she was too weak to help. She'd chosen Rachel, because she should have been lighter, but handling a nearly unconscious patient wasn't easy.

'Can I get some help?' Her voice strained as she tried to heave Rachel over the rim of the tub.

A tall figure appeared at her side. She didn't need to look to know who it was, but as he spoke, her heart skipped a beat.

'I've got her. You get your butt out of here.' Nick reached into the bathtub and lifted the petite woman out with little effort. Gently, he laid her over his shoulder, held her legs close to his chest and ran as flames licked through the bathroom door from the inside.

Jenny's legs buckled. Stumbling, she almost fell before hands reached out for her. Jenny recognised Mrs B.'s daughter Rebecca.

'You're quite the wonder woman, aren't you! I can see what he likes about you.' Jenny's mind spun almost as much as her vision. The comment struck a chord. Had Nick spoken about her to his childhood sweetheart?

Not now!

The commotion of people working frantically around them made it impossible for Jenny to respond. Rebecca helped her stumble further from the blaze.

William Creek Pub was miles from any water source. Mrs B.'s son Mick, along with a handful of able bodies tried to put the fire out until Jenny and Philips pulled Rachel and Curtis out. Now the occupants were safe, it was obvious the little amount of water wasn't going to be enough.

A sea of faces, covered in soot, sweat and red dust watched as the fire continued to ravage the buildings. One by one, walls collapsed, dust rose, and the roof caved in.

Jenny sat with Rebecca in the dirt, surveying the burning units. 'Such a shame.'

'Not really.' Rebecca grinned. 'I hated those bloody old buildings anyway.' The fire illuminated Rebecca's face and Jenny wondered if they might eventually become friends.

She snapped her head back to her job. 'I better check on my witnesses and get them somewhere safe. Thanks for the help.'

Rebecca rose to her feet, nodded and busied herself dusting off her shorts.

A small group of people hovered by the police Landcruiser. Jenny joined them. Rachel was resting against the wheel of the vehicle. Curtis was beginning to stir, his head resting on her lap.

'We need to get these two out of here Philips.'

Nick gaped at her. 'Was this intentional?' He waved his hand toward the still burning building.

'We believe so.'

Jenny didn't want to say too much with people milling around them. Besides, she didn't want to draw Nick into another dangerous situation. The last time he was shot and she would never forgive herself if anything happened to him again. He was all his younger brother Sam had now that his mother was gone and his dad was dead.

Curtis was now sitting up, a bottle of water in his hand, his hair hanging over his face as he put his head between his knees to recover. Rachel shivered as shock set in. They needed to be inside, safe and recovered enough to answer her questions. And there were a lot of questions.

'I need to get these two back to Coober Pedy.'

'That's a long drive for two fire victims. Even if they look alright now, smoke inhalation should be taken seriously. Why don't you get them back to my place to recover first?'

'That's not a good idea Nick.' A vision of Nick bleeding out on Murphy's floor made her shudder.

'Why? They aren't harmed enough to call in the Flying Doctors, but they need rest before you drive them all the way back to town.' Nick studied Jenny's face, then turned to Philips hoping sense would prevail.

Philips frowned. 'What's going on?'

'Load them into the car Philips. I'll be with you in a second.' Jenny pulled Nick away from prying eyes, her arm linked through his. He glanced over his shoulder as Philips helped Curtis to his feet. His gaze lingered on her hand on his arm, then shifted to her clothing, before resting on her eyes.

'You're not in uniform, but you've got your vest on?'

'We got an urgent call. There wasn't enough time to get changed.'

'These two a danger to anyone?' He gazed back as Philips opened the back door of the police Landcruiser and ushered Rachel and Curtis inside.

'No. But they are both in danger – witnesses in a case I'm working on.'

'That woman at the BnS?' His eyebrows rose with the realisation.

'Yes. While I appreciate the offer Nick, I don't want you getting shot again.'

'And I don't want you driving back to town, with someone out there keen on taking these two out,' he waved over his shoulder, 'accidentally getting you instead.'

She didn't mention someone already tried. Her mind raced with excuses, but none of them was good for her or her witnesses. There were weapons at Nick's place. They would be alright.

'Okay. We'll stay at your place until I can get safe passage for them back to town. But you and Sam stay out of any trouble. Got that!'

Nick smiled at her finger, waving in front of his face before saluting. 'Got it M'am!' She slapped his hand away from his forehead. His stupid grin remained.

'Really! You need to promise me. I have nightmares about you bleeding out on Murphy's timber floor you know.' Nick's face turned serious a moment. She hated having to force his smile away – it was something she relished and he seldom did. But now wasn't the time.

'I'll keep Sam out of trouble, but if anything goes astray and you need back up, I'm not about to sit idly by and ignore it.'

She knew there was no arguing with him. Taking a slow breath, she decided not answering was her best option.

'Ready!' Philips called from the driver's seat of the Police vehicle.

'You can ride with me.' Nick ushered her with a gentle hand on her back. She stopped outside Philips' door.

'We're heading to William Creek Station. We can get these two cleaned up, fed and make sure there are no medical complications before we drive them to town.'

'Do we get a say in this?' Curtis sat in the back seat, his arm wrapped protectively around Rachel's shoulder.

'No. You've done a bang-up job of getting both of you in harm's way already. You just sit back, shut up and hopefully we'll get you back to town alive.'

Philips chuckled. 'Seriously though. I feel better with you two riding shotgun.'

'Okay. Nick and I'll ride behind. You lead the way. Pull around the front and wait for us to get Nick's ute.'

As Jenny rushed to the front of the pub, she couldn't shake the feeling of still being watched. Chiding herself, she shook the fear off. They were in the middle of nowhere. If a black Audi pulled up in front of the pub, she would have noticed.

Chapter 37

Her mobile phone pinged in her pocket as she opened the passenger's side of Nick's ute. 'Is Sam coming with us?'

'No. He came in his own car tonight.'

'What were you two doing here at the pub?' He slid into the seat, the smell of his aftershave lingered over the fire and ash.

'Dinner.' There was a moment of silence. Nick slid behind the wheel, his door still open, biting his lip. 'And I found something the other day.' He pulled the door closed and turned to study her.

'Something that might help our investigations?'

'Too early to tell.' He started the engine. 'I was going over it with Rebecca when the fire started.'

'What did you find?' She sat back in the seat, pulling the seatbelt on and clipping it as tension rose in her neck. Her stomach tumbled and fluttered.

'Honestly. I'm not sure.' Philips drove around the corner of the pub. 'It was an old ledger but not like our usual guest registration book. No vehicle registration numbers, no guests' signatures, just numbers and initials.'

'And you've never seen anything like it before?'

'Never. But I know it's from the station. The handwriting is mostly mum's but dad's is in there too. No one else. I thought Rebecca might have seen it at some stage and known what it was all about.'

'And had she?'

'No, but we were going over it when all hell broke loose.'

'Do you have it with you?'

'No. Sorry. I left it with Rebecca.'

Nick flashed his lights to let Philips know he was ready. The police vehicle pulled out of the parking area, onto the Oodnadatta road. No one would have guessed the narrow strip of dirt was the desert highway and linked major stations, truck stops and tourist destinations through the red centre of Australia.

'Damn. I would have liked to get a look at it.'

'I'll grab it tomorrow, when you've got your witnesses back to town safely.' Nick glanced into his rear-view mirror as they caught up to Philips. 'You're still coming out sometime this weekend?'

'That is the plan.' Nick glanced into the mirror again, his face illuminated by the dashboard lights was confused. 'What's up?'

'Could be nothing.' He checked again but said nothing.

'But?' Jenny turned to see over her shoulder as headlights raced up behind them. 'Look out!'

Her neck flung forward, then back, hitting the seat with enough force to make her neck crack. Their vehicle slid sideways a moment, but Nick recovered it quickly, putting his foot on the accelerator to gain some distance.

'A friend of yours?' Nick kept checking the mirror as he navigated the rough dirt road.

'He must be off his tree.' Jenny's phone vibrated, a reminder she needed to read her earlier text message. Nick flashed his lights to get Philips' attention. He sped up behind him, trying to avoid the pursuing vehicle. Nick's radio squelched inaudibly on the dashboard. Jenny reached for the handset.

'Philips. We've got company. Put a little juice into it mate.' The Police Landcruiser pulled away. The radio remained silent. Headlights hit the rear-view mirror again, but this time Nick was ready for it.

He dropped a gear on his V8, let the clutch go and slammed his foot on the accelerator. The vehicle pursued them, giving them no room for escape. Nick's car came into a bend too fast, sliding up into the verge, shrubs torn to pieces as his tyres fought for grip. Jenny grabbed the handle above her passenger door, holding tight as the four-wheel drive gained traction and jumped back down the embankment to the road.

'Is this guy armed?' Nick's eyes were wide as he peered into the rear-view mirror again.

'Most likely, but he usually prefers fire to guns. At least that's the MO so far.' The vehicle hit them in the rear once more. Nick's knuckles gripped the steering wheel. Jenny watched Philips race ahead, disappearing into the dust making it difficult for Nick to see where he was going.

The advantage was, it was almost certainly worse for Newman.

'Hold on to something. Tight!' Jenny grabbed the dash with one hand, the side handle with the other as Nick accelerated. The vehicle behind sped up, headlights disappearing below the back of the ute. Nick hit the brakes – hard, locking them up a moment before the ABS kicked in. The slam at the rear of the vehicle nearly threw Jenny's butt out of her seat, her head snapped forward.

'Hopefully that will slow him down.' Nick dropped the gears down again, pressed the accelerator to the floor and sped away. Jenny swung around to see one broken headlight slowly disappearing into the distance.

'That won't stop him. He'll limp along. He likely knows who you are Nick.' Jenny studied her phone. There was no reception, but the dings were two missed text messages. She opened them, hoping they would be visible without reception.

Both text messages were from O'Connell. The first one made her gasp.

*Got the army service records for Newman –
dishonourable discharge. Failed his psych evaluation. He's a
loose cannon. Be careful!*

But the second message left her speechless.

Chapter 38

Jenny reached for the radio handset, pressed the button and glanced over as Nick peered into the rear-view mirror for one final check before she spoke.

'Philips. Let's get to the homestead ASAP.'

'Roger that!'

'How are your passengers?'

'Scared, but safe.'

'I've got a message from the O'Connell. Keep your head down. Okay.' Nick's gaze shifted to her, then back on the road as they raced toward the dust cloud left by Philips ahead. The headlights shone into the mist of red dirt. Nick steadied his pace.

'Will do.'

'What's up?' Nick watched her place the radio handset back on the clip.

'I'll need to phone O'Connell when I get to your place. This guy was thrown out of the army for failing his psychiatric evaluation after returning from Afghanistan.'

'That's not surprising. That place would have been bloody awful. He's likely not the only one.'

'No. But he's probably on a short list when it comes to accusations of torture.'

'Probably not as uncommon as you think.' Nick was remarkably calm for someone who minutes ago outran a nutter who might be a murderer.

'That's a sad thought. I'll get the details from O'Connell when we get to the Homestead, but either way, O'Connell said he's a loose cannon and to be on the lookout. After nearly getting rammed off the road, I think we can confirm his assessment was dead right.'

'That's if our pursuer was the guy you think he is.'

'True.'

They slowed as they turned off the main road, into the station entrance. The faded signage wasn't visible in the darkness, but Jenny was familiar with it now.

'Do you want to give me a bit of background, or is this an ongoing investigation?'

Jenny smiled. It was her go-to line when she didn't want to talk shop with him, or even Nev.

'It's an ongoing case, but since it's ended up on your doorstep, I'd say it's fair you get some background.' She thought about where to start as they drove up toward the homestead. It looked stately, silhouetted by the full moon, with the escarpment behind.

'We believe the fire victim was accidentally targeted. The killer was after Rachel.' She pointed to the police vehicle parked outside the homestead. Philips stepped out, put his hand up in front of the passenger's side door to stop Curtis and Rachel from getting out. He pulled his service revolver and surveyed the area, his eyes resting on Jenny through the windscreen.

Her pulse rushed in her ears. Sweat stuck to the back of her shirt and under her arms. 'I'll go over it all inside. I need to interview Rachel and Curtis. You should listen in.'

'Okay.' Nick opened the door and turned to step out. She reached for his arm.

'Stay here a second.' He frowned. 'Please!'

'Okay.' She nodded, let go of his arm and opened her door. Retrieving her gun, she joined Philips. 'I'll do a sweep inside. You watch them.' She stepped away, then turned back. 'All of them.' She nodded toward Nick.

'You got it.' Philips gave her a thumbs up.

Gun ready, Jenny stalked toward the darkened building. The moonlight cast a glow, just enough to show the way to the familiar pathway leading to the veranda.

Two steps up the porch, she searched for the door handle under the darkened veranda.

Opening the door, she cringed as her first footfalls inside made the old floorboards creak.

Slowly she stalked down the hall, turning on the lights as she entered each room. First, the formal living, then the dining, on down the hall, past the grand staircase into the new kitchen, living area.

Satisfied downstairs was clear, she called from the front door. 'Bring them in and then give me a hand to clear upstairs.'

It was unlikely anyone made it to Nick's house before them, but Newman wasn't working alone. She knew Hayes was his partner, but how far was the woman willing to go to protect her backside? She had her own detective on a leash, so Jenny hoped murder wasn't her game. But it was someone's.

Nick entered, then Rachel and Curtis, with Philips herding the group from behind, eyes alert.

'I'll take them through to the kitchen. Settle them with a drink.' Nick waved his hand for Rachel and Curtis to follow him.

'Upstairs.' Philips nodded. Jenny tiptoed toward the stringy-bark timber staircase, Philips close behind, her weapon still drawn and ready. She placed her foot on the first step, then the next. As her foot fell on the third, a thud from above made her jump. Glancing back, she saw Philips' face mirror hers.

Chapter 39

Taking another wary step, Jenny almost lost balance as a grey and tan tabby cat dropped at her feet, purring and twitching its tail. Supressing a nervous curse, she exhaled with a loud puff of her cheeks. Philips chuckled nervously under his breath.

'Let's get this done,' she whispered. 'I've got news from O'Connell.'

'Sounds ominous,' he whispered back.

'It's worse than we thought.'

'Not making me feel any better.'

They reached the top of the stairs and began clearing each room one by one. Jenny knew the first room well. It was where she stayed when she visited. The large bed was soft, the furniture old, the smell of mothballs lingered.

The next room was Nick's. She could recognise the smell of his aftershave a mile away. Having never been in his room, clearing it now was strange, like she was invading his privacy.

Across the hall, Philips called to say Sam's room was clear. The homestead was large. There was another wing to clear yet, but so far there was no sign anyone or anything was out of place.

Ten minutes later, they made their way downstairs. The smell of coffee made her stomach gurgle. Philips laughed. Nick smiled.

'You hungry?'

'I'm always hungry. You know that.' She plonked down at the long table where Rachel and Curtis sat, huddled together like naughty school children. 'Okay you two. Time to come clean before I arrest you.'

Philips sat opposite the couple; his stare spoke volumes. Curtis's nostrils flared. Rachel closed her eyes, holding back tears.

'Arrest us! What the hell for? Someone tried to burn us alive.' Curtis poked his finger at the table like he was barking out orders.

'Let me make myself perfectly clear. You!' She pointed to exaggerate the fact she held Curtis accountable for this whole mess. 'You decided to blackmail a lawyer and a nut-job ex-army corporal. Why didn't you take the evidence to Smart, or the police? What the hell were you thinking?'

'He wasn't, obviously.' Nick passed her a drink and opened a packet of potato chips before pouring them in a bowl.

'I've just been notified by my Senior that Michael Newman is a returned, discharged army explosives expert with a poor psychiatric report. An on top of that, he was discharged for charges of torture and arson, and your friend Ms Hayes ensured he was never tried for war crimes.'

'We don't know anything about that.' Rachel's voice quivered as she spoke.

'Tell us what you do know then. Maybe we can get you safely back to town, into the hospital for a check-up and home, without pressing charges. Maybe!'

'I was Hayes's PA.' Jenny nodded she knew. 'I found files, but I also booked her airfares.'

'We found the files. Luckily, it was us and not Newman. What airfares?'

'To Dubai for the most part, but I know, from her expenses, she booked flights out of Dubai to Afghanistan, all coinciding with adoptions to wealthy families in Melbourne.'

'So you are saying that with each of the files we have copies of,' Jenny's eyes grew wide. 'Hayes flew in and out of

Afghanistan? She was the one smuggling the children, not Newman?'

'I know who he is. I met him a few times at work functions and then when he consulted with Ms Hayes on his case. I'm not sure what part he played in the adoptions.'

'I've got a good idea how involved he was, but I need to know if either of you saw him in Coober Pedy or at the BnS the night Melinda was killed?'

'I never saw him in town, just his car.' Rachel reached for the glass Nick offered.

'How do you know it was his car?'

'Everyone at work knew Mr Newman gave his son a company car when he got back from Afghanistan.'

Jenny's mind was racing. Anyone could have been driving Newman's car around town. 'I need to call O'Connell.' She pushed her chair back to rise. 'You have a phone I can use? Privately?'

Nick pointed back toward the front of the house. 'My office is back this way.' He led the way. She followed close behind, her head spinning. Newman spoke the language. No doubt he organised the children, but were they orphans? Did Hayes even care?

'Keep an eye out Nick and tell Philips to do the same. This guy is unpredictable. We need to get these two into town now, rather than wait until morning. They should be good enough to travel.' Nick nodded, switched on the office light and pointed to the phone.

'You calling for back up?'

'No. I'm calling to bring O'Connell up to date. Can you let Philips know we'll move out as soon as I'm done?' He nodded and turned to leave.

She rubbed her temples. All the pieces of information, flooding into her brain at once like a pressure cooker, waiting to explode. Marj's comments about Roberts moving in with Hayes in her motel suite. The fact he wouldn't let them speak with her because she was a witness in a Harlequins investigation. The injury at the hospital and how he recognised her phone number on Nev's caller ID.

She dialled Penny's mobile, hoping her friend would have the answers she needed to finally put the pieces of this puzzle together.

Chapter 40

Jenny hung up, her heart racing. She was going out on a limb, with only circumstantial evidence to support her theory. Would O'Connell back her? It was a huge risk and one she hoped wouldn't ruin her career.

But solving this case. Saving Rachel and Curtis from harm – that was her priority today.

She dialled another number and waited. Two rings, then O'Connell's voice sounded on the end of the line. His tone was forced calm.

'O'Connell speaking.'

'Sir.'

'Williams. Where the hell have you been?'

'Taking cover at William Creek Station Sir. We got to the pub and found Rachel and Curtis's room on fire.'

'I heard. Mrs B. called it in. We are too short-staffed to send a unit out right now, but is everyone okay?'

'They both have some smoke inhalation, but they'll be alright. There's no tank oxygen out here even if I wanted to administer it and I'm not calling in the Royal Flying Doctors when we have a nutter on the loose. Whoever lit the fire, tried to run us off the road on the way to Nick's place.'

'What's your plan?'

She sucked in a breath. 'What you told me about Newman's military record, it fits with his civilian record. The guy's almost certainly a serial arsonist, and probably our killer, but all our evidence is circumstantial Sir. We have nothing solid. Rachel said she found those adoption documents and she knows Hayes flew to Dubai, then booked internal flights that she thought Rachel wouldn't find. Hayes was in Afghanistan during the lead up to each of those adoptions Sir.'

'I'll need immigration to confirm that.'

'We need to get a warrant for her phone records too.'

'I can't get a warrant issued while Major Crimes are covering her arse.'

'I know Sir. I think I might have worked out a way around that.' She outlined her plan, then waited for the big fat NO she expected, but didn't come.

'I'll grab Sarge. We'll both be at the station by the time you get there.'

'Thanks Sir.'

'Don't thank me yet. If this goes pear-shaped, I'll deny everything.'

Jenny laughed, unsure if he was being serious or not. As the phone went silent, she suspected he was quite serious.

Returning to the kitchen, she picked up the tail-end of the conversation. Philips was asking Curtis where Melinda fitted into the picture.

'Melinda was my friend,' Rachel answered. 'She offered to bring me here, to be with Curtis. To be safe.'

'That didn't go to plan. How did Newman know you would be here?' Philips glanced up as Jenny spoke, his eyes questioning. She shook her head gently to signal she wouldn't explain in front of their two witnesses.

'I have no idea. Melinda might have told her dad, who possibly told Samantha, but why would she want Melinda dead? She's known us for years, but Melinda was her boss's daughter. She went to her birthday parties, staff Christmas parties. How could she?'

'Maybe Newman acted alone?' Philips offered in obvious consolation.

'I don't think so.' Jenny interrupted. 'Can I talk with you a second Philips?' She needed to brief him before they loaded up to go back to Coober Pedy. A broken headlight and possible busted radiator weren't enough to keep their pursuer away for long. Whoever tried to run them off the road was likely not too far way. They needed to get going.

'Damn!' The smell of smoke made Jenny turn to the front door. Tendrils of grey floated under the front door. 'The back doors.'

Nick rushed toward the sliding glass doors as an explosion shook the glass and a wall of flames rose. 'He's made a pyre out of hay.'

'Newman is an army explosives expert. This place is stone, right?'

'It's got timber in the top floor and the roof.'

'Okay! The basement.'

'There's no way out of there and help is too far away.' Nick shook his head.

'We can't run out the front, we'll be sitting ducks.'

Jenny turned at the sound of Rachel sobbing. She wanted to say it was going to be okay – that they'd get out of this mess, but she couldn't. Her throat tightened.

'Follow me.' Nick rushed out of the kitchen, into the hallway. Jenny waved for Philips to grab Rachel and Curtis, before following.

Another explosion rocked the old stone building. Jenny ducked instinctively, but nothing fell from the ceiling.

Stopping, she looked behind to see Rachel shaking, Curtis trying to coax her with a gentle tug of her arm. 'Hurry up you two.' She rushed back to usher them forward, as Philips encouraged from behind.

'We can't go up. We'll be trapped.' Curtis stopped at the bottom of the staircase, frowning at Nick's retreating figure.

'If Nick says go up, we go up. It's his house. He knows what he's doing.' Jenny stepped in front of Curtis and raced up the stairs two at a time.

Chapter 41

Nick waited a few steps down the wide, carpeted hallway. Smoke filled the roofline, making Jenny duck to get fresh air. Her hands shook, her chest tightened as visions of the shed fire flooded back.

'Follow Nick.' She pushed Curtis, then Rachel past before waiting on Philips who glared at her, an unasked question in his eyes. He wanted to know where they were going. Why Nick was leading them upstairs. She didn't have an answer for him.

Instead, she pushed her partner forward with a slap on the back. 'Let's go.' Pushing her own anxiety aside, she followed.

'In here.' Nick opened a spare guest room. Holding the door, he ushered everyone inside. A glow of fire shone through sheer curtains. Smoke filtered out of cracks and crevices in the ceiling. The old building wasn't draft proof, and every tiny hole was allowing in fumes.

Nick rushed to the wardrobe door, opening it wide, revealing a spiral staircase. 'Staff access.' He answered Jenny's raised eyebrows. 'It leads to the outside, on the shearing-shed side. Get to the shed.' The lights flickered.

'Then what?'

'Then we get out of here, back to town.'

'What about the house?'

A roof timber gave way, the ceiling fell in with a crash. Smoke, dust and debris billowed into the room.

'The boys are out on a muster. There's no on here to save it. It's only a house Jenny.' He pushed her inside the doorway – into pitch blackness.

'Move down, quickly, but carefully.' She called into the cavern. The timber staircase was solid under foot, despite the number of people descending all at once.

Philips opened the doorway below, allowing a glimmer of moonlight mixed with firelight to filter in. The smoke danced with an eerie rhythm all around them, making her aware of the amount of smoke inhalation they were all taking in. Fear for Rachel and Curtis crept under her skin. They were already exposed to smoke. What if it became too much?

She squeezed past as they exited, ready to take the lead. A quick glance over her shoulder ensured Nick was out. Her pulse raced. The shearing shed was a few hundred metres from the main homestead. She started to run.

The moonlight provided limited vision, but the flames from the burning homestead cast a glow across the night sky. Navigation was still difficult. Jenny knew her way around Nick's home, but the shearing sheds were a mystery.

Her heart pounded in her chest as she turned the makeshift timber lock on the worn wooden door. The old nail and block of timber made her smile, despite the anxiety.

She ushered Philips and her witnesses inside, then entered. 'What now?' She turned to face Nick as he pulled the door closed.

'Now we get the old truck from the rear of the shearing yards.'

'A truck!'

'The cattle truck is all that's left, unless you think we can ram five people into the chopper.'

'We could try and get back to the cars.'

'That's too risky.' Philips joined their huddled conversation.

'He's right.' Nick sucked in a breath through his nostrils. Jenny realised he was bracing for an argument. She wasn't known for her cool temper and the more stressful the situation, the more likely she was to push against common sense.

'Okay. Truck it is,' she conceded.

'Can I grab your torch?' Nick held his hand out.

Jenny pulled it from her utility vest. 'Here.' She found his hand in the darkness. Her skin tingled at his touch.

The torch flicked to life. Jenny turned to Philips behind her. 'Philips, grab yours out and follow us.'

'You got it. You two, follow me.' Philips clicked the torch on and flashed the beam to where Rachel and Curtis huddled, their eyes wide, like deer in headlights.

Jenny followed Nick's torchlight to the rear of the building where a beam of light struck an old worn tyre before the vehicle came into full view. Far from the bigrig she expected – the faded red paint and rusted old Bedford tray top truck almost made her laugh. They were never going to all squeeze into the cab and top speed was probably less than eighty kilometres an hour.

'You're kidding right! That thing probably needs a crank start.'

'Or a push,' Nick offered.

Did she see a grin on his face?

'You choose now to find a sense of humour?'

'Better than not at all.' He opened the cab. 'Philips, you and Curtis get in the back. I'll take the girls in the front.'

'Got it.' He nodded, then encouraged Curtis to climb into the metal stock crate at the rear. 'Hold on tight mate. It's going to be a rough ride.'

Jenny opened the passenger's side door with an effort. It creaked loudly as she ushered Rachel inside. Hoisting herself up using the rusted foot step, she forced the door closed with a loud grunt and two hands as Nick turned the motor over.

'Come on Girl. You can do it.' Nick coaxed as the motor turned over again. He pumped the pedal a few times, held it flat to the floor and turned the key again as everyone held their breath.

The motor fired. Jenny wanted to cheer, instead, she wriggled back and forth in her seat willing the truck forward. Another explosion rocked the tin on the shearing shed. The sound of rushing air made Jenny wonder if the bulk gas tanks just went up.

Nick crunched the truck into gear. Lurching forward, he pushed it into second gear, then third as they drew around the rear of the shed toward the track. The beautiful, stately homestead came into view – fully ablaze now.

'I'm sorry.' She offered Nick a consoling smile as he double-d'd the clutch for fourth gear and steered the ancient truck towards town. Jenny saw his face as he peered into his rear-view mirror. For all the bravado about it only being a house, she could see the pain in his eyes.

His father died there. His mother raised him in that house and now, everything he and Sam owned was up in smoke. She hoped the basement, where all the family history lay, would survive.

Guilt nudged at her conscience. She didn't want the cellar contents saved only for Nick's sake, but for herself and her family. Because so far, Nick's place was the only connection to what happened to her cousin and aunt.

She shook herself back to reality as the truck bounced along the dirt track. A final look behind allowed her some peace of mind. They weren't being followed. Not this time.

'We've got two hours or more to get to the bottom of this Rachel. Start at the beginning.'

Chapter 42

A jolt rocked Jenny's head into the truck window. Her eyes snapped open.

'Nearly there.' Nick's voice sounded safe and warm, making her wish she sat in the middle instead of Rachel.

'I'm sorry. I shouldn't have fallen asleep.'

'It's alright. You've had a busy week, and tonight was crazy.'

'This whole case is crazy.'

'You'll figure it out.'

'Thanks for the vote of confidence.' She watched him focus on the road. Rachel stirred next to her.

'Can you drop us off at the station, thanks?'

'Sure.'

She couldn't be sure, but for a moment, she thought Nick sounded offended. Maybe he was. He helped save her witnesses. And her. His place was destroyed in the process and she was fobbing him off.

'I'm sorry about your house. I'll call Tim and Nev. You can crash in my room tonight, but I've got work to do.'

'Thanks. But I'll go see Marj at the motel.'

Was it her bed he didn't want to sleep in? The thought of Nick in her bed made her blush.

She was thankful it was still too dark for him to see.

'If you're sure.'

'As much as I appreciate the offer. I don't feel comfortable sleeping in your bed.'

Rachel was wide awake now. She glanced from Jenny to Nick and grinned. 'He means without you in it.'

Nick coughed. Jenny cleared her throat. 'You said you never met the guy with the tattoos before, right?'

'Right. Not before Friday night at the BnS.'

'Did Curtis know him?'

'No. He said the guy arrived the day before, all scary and mean. Made threats about keeping our mouths shut and told us to hand over the evidence and disappear or we might end up dead.'

'I see.' Jenny glanced at Nick over Rachel's head. His eyes were on the road, but she could see he was listening.

She thought there was something not right about Roberts and now, with Rachel's information and Penny's analysis of the truck, she was fairly certain she knew what was going on. Now all she needed to do was get some evidence and convince her bosses.

The truck pulled up slowly outside the station. Nick parked it away from the front doors. 'I'll head over to the motel. If you need anything, call. Okay!'

Jenny jumped down, held the door for Rachel and watched as Philips and Curtis climbed stiffly from the rear of the truck.

'Nice ride.' She patted Philips on the back as he leant over to stretch.

'That was bloody awful.' His eyes searched the deserted street as he stretched his back. He glanced at his watch. 'Three a.m.. No wonder I'm stuffed.'

The lights were on at the station. Jenny waved Rachel and Curtis to the front doors. 'Let's get you two inside. Where it's safe.'

Inside, O'Connell manned the counter, Sergeant Mackenzie nowhere in sight. 'Is the boss in?'

'In his office, trying to get us a warrant.'

'Philips, can you make these two comfortable? See if we can organise some food too?' O'Connell indicated for him to lead their witnesses out of earshot.

Philips nodded and obliged, his limbs moving slowly. He grabbed at his hamstring, cramp making him limp.

'Ask for access to Roberts' phone records while you are at it.' 'Roberts?' O'Connell peered over his reading glasses.

'Yes. I think we've been chasing the wrong man. Any idea where Roberts is right now?'

'No. What have you found out?'

'Penny told me there wasn't enough MDMA in her testing of the truck debris to indicate it was a lab after all.'

'So.'

'So Roberts told you there wasn't any Harlequin drug trade in town, but he told me the reason he came here was to manage a drug lab for the Harlequins. He said he was at the hospital because there was an altercation with his gang about losing the truck and the lab in the fire, but….'

'If the truck wasn't a lab then he was lying.'

'Right, and I think he was in a fight with Newman?'

'We've got Newman's phone records sorted. They're on the desk.' Jenny and O'Connell rushed to the shared workstation.

'Here.' He handed her a pile of paperwork.

Thumbing through she found the phone call log. Running her finger down the page she stopped, reached for a yellow highlighter and began marking numbers.

'Hayes.' She used the yellow pen. 'But this one…' She reached for another colour, choosing orange and removing the lid she marked another mobile number. 'This is Roberts' burner.'

'How do you know?'

'It's a hunch, but we can find out where the SIM card was purchased, can't we?'

'I'll organise it.' O'Connell lifted the handset of the desk phone as Sergeant Mackenzie's door slammed open.

'Bloody bureaucratic bullshit.'

'I take it we can't get Hayes's credit-card records?' Jenny expected the Major Crimes task force would make their life difficult.

'No, but we got Newman's. They are being sent through now.'

Jenny scurried to the front counter computer and opened the email account. 'You look shocking Williams.'

'You should see Philips. He rode in the back of a stock crate to get here.'

'What the hell?'

'Long story, but we were cornered and abandoned the Police vehicle at Nick's place. Whoever wanted Rachel and Curtis dead, also burned Nick's house down.'

O'Connell hung up. 'Shit. That's crappy. I wondered why you were all covered in soot, but you said you pulled Rachel and Curtis out of the motel fire.' He shrugged.

'It's been a long night Sir. But we need to finish this one, before Rachel and Curtis get hurt.'

'The SIM card was purchased locally. I'll call the newsagency as soon as they open and see if we can get footage.'

'What's going on?' Sergeant Mackenzie frowned.

'Williams noticed this number; a burner phone has been calling Hayes.'

'And Newman.' Jenny tapped the open phone record on her computer screen. 'I think it's Roberts Sir and I think we need to get a warrant for his credit-cards and other financials.'

'That's not going to happen.'

'Maybe if we have probable cause Sir?

'Explain!'

'Roberts said he came to town with the Harlequins, but I think he came with or for Hayes.'

'Didn't we decide Newman is Hayes's lacky?'

'He is, was.'

'Was?'

'I think he's dead Sir.'

Sergeant Mackenzie laughed aloud. 'Where do you get that idea? He's been burning down half of the town.'

'No Sir. I think we've been led to believe he is. Penny found evidence in the debris from the fire I only found out about last night.' She checked her watch. 'Or was it this morning?' She shook her head.

'Either way, it's taken Penny a while to sift through everything, but there wasn't enough MDMA in the truck to be a lab. It was likely planted on the doors to make us think it was a lab. The band members all deny having anything to do with drugs. They have no record to substantiate a drug history. According to Rachel, she and Curtis met Roberts the day before the BnS when Roberts warned them off blackmailing Hayes and told them to hand over the evidence.'

'That's all news, but it doesn't explain why you think Newman is dead.'

She pulled up the rest of his phone and credit-card records. 'Because of what Penny told me and these records Sir.' She stepped aside so O'Connell and her Sergeant could see.

O'Connell's eyebrow questioned Sarge, who slowly drew a deep breath, his chest rising with frustration. 'Get on with it Williams. This isn't Murder She Wrote.'

'Sorry Sir.' She was enjoying the reveal, but her boss was right. 'Newman hasn't used his credit-card or made a call since last Saturday Sir. Hayes and Robert's burner, if I'm right and I think I am, haven't tried to call him since then either. There was also burnt flesh in the truck debris and it wasn't Melinda's Sir.'

'So you think Newman was killed in the truck fire?'

'I think his body was disposed of, in the fire. I think Melinda might have been killed because she saw it, not because she knew about Rachel's evidence.'

Mackenzie rubbed his chin as O'Connell whistled. 'Do we have DNA confirmation from McGregor yet?'

'No Sarge. If we did, we wouldn't be having this conversation. We'd be hauling Roberts and Hayes in here.'

'We can't arrest either without some serious evidence. This is all just circumstantial.' O'Connell rubbed his hand through his thick hair as he spoke, his eyes darting from Jenny to Sarge, waiting for someone to come up with an idea.

'We are almost certain Newman is dead. We have evidence to link Newman with the illegal adoption. Roberts knew my personal mobile, which Philips gave Hayes, so he must have gotten it from her. We know Roberts was staying in Hayes's motel room and according to Marj, the relationship wasn't platonic.'

Jenny thumbed each finger as she listed off the facts.

'When did she say that?'

'She alluded to it when she said he checked in. She never saw anyone matching Newman's description in Hayes's room and I canvassed the town with Michael Newman's photo. No one saw him.'

'What about the Audi driver?'

'Dark tinted windows. It's Newman's dad's car, but we have no evidence Newman was driving. The band knew Curtis and Rachel had something on Hayes, but they didn't know what. Maybe they thought Hayes and her tattooed friend would harm them?'

'Damn!' Sarge tapped his fingers on the desk. 'How are we going to prove any of this?'

Jenny grinned as she glanced from Sarge to O'Connell. They were as excited as kids at Christmas. It was good working with the team on this, instead of trying to figure out everything on her own.

She wondered again if she should come clean about why she took the job, but forced her personal agenda to the back of her mind. Now wasn't the time.

'We might be able to get that warrant if we can confirm Roberts purchased this SIM.'

O'Connell glanced at his watch. 'The newsagent will be open in a few hours. I'll get onto them as soon as the doors open.'

'Well, while we wait for that, I'll get my uniform on and see if I can track our detective friend down.'

'Be careful Williams. He's pulled the wool over our eyes. He's a canny one and if he gets any idea you suspect him... well, you know. Just be careful.' Sergeant Mackenzie didn't make eye-contact, instead, he turned and strode back to his office.

For a moment, Jenny studied his closed door. She turned to O'Connell, who shrugged, but the grin on his face said he was thinking the same thing as her. Sergeant Mackenzie was finally warming to the new girl in town.

Chapter 43

The night was warm, but the morning sunrise brought another level of heat with it. Jenny knew she should have gone home to bed. Philips left Rachel and Curtis with O'Connell and Sarge, to do just that, but she wouldn't be able to catch a wink.

The motel was beginning to stir as Jenny wandered over to the restaurant. The early morning breakfast buffet was calling her name.

The cool air greeted her as she opened the double glass doors. The smell of filtered coffee lured her in. She preferred a coffee from her favourite barista, but drip-filtered coffee would have to do. Her head spun with so much work to get through.

'Hey Jenny.' Cheryl smiled from behind the bar. 'You look zonked.'

'I am.'

Her face was already wiped clean of any residue from the fires the night before, but the smell lingered in her hair and she knew there were dark rings under her eyes from lack of sleep.

'Hard week?'

'Very. But I it's looking up now.'

'It's Friday, you'd hope so.'

'That doesn't mean anything when we're working on a case out here. I could be on this one all weekend.'

'That sucks.' Cheryl picked up the EFTPOS machine. 'You here for breakfast?'

'Yep.' Jenny pulled her credit-card from the front pocket of her uniform and held it aloft, ready to tap the machine.

'So's your friend.' Cheryl grinned and nodded her head toward the back corner of the restaurant.

Jenny frowned, then turned to see what Cheryl meant.

In the corner, behind the concertina doors dividing the restaurant from the bar sat Nick, a plate full of hot breakfast in front of him.

Jenny glanced back at Cheryl whose smile grew wider. The woman was a closed book until recently. Now, she often joined her, Nev and Tim for drinks or dinner.

'You should join him.'

'I might just do that.' Jenny pulled her card back as the machine dinged to say the payment was processed. She turned, strolling casually for Nick's table, hoping he wasn't sick of the sight of her after last night.

'Hey. Do you want company?'

Nick half stood. 'Of course. Why wouldn't I?' He pointed to the chair on his left before picking up his knife and fork again.

'I don't know. Maybe the crazy cop who got your house burnt down might not be number one on your breakfast buddy list.'

Nick stared at her a moment, his fork halfway to his mouth. 'I know we started out rough. I was a right dick. But I thought we were past that. I've been pretty straight up since then.'

Jenny sat down. Nick's tone was serious. She went to say she was only joking, but he kept speaking.

'When that fire started, all I could think about was getting you to safety. Not Danny, not your witnesses, just you Jenny Williams.' He put the forkful of food in his mouth and chewed with unexpected force.

'I'm sorry. I didn't want to make you feel....' She thought about it a moment. How did he feel? What was he saying?

'It's fine. Grab your breakfast. You must be as starved as I am.'

And the conversation was over. Just like that. Nick was back to his usual self. Emotions buried under his tough guy façade. She sucked a sharp breath through her nostrils, pushed the chair back, her hands firmly planted on the table ready to rise.

Nick's hand wrapped around hers.

'I'm sorry. I'm pretty crap at this. You being a cop scares the hell out of me. Especially when people are trying to burn you alive. I'm not good at this stuff.'

Jenny smiled at his discomfort. 'What stuff?' She didn't sit, she didn't move closer even though every fibre of her being desperately wanted to.

'You know what stuff. At least I hope you do.' He let her hand go.

She sat back down, leaning in toward him, her lips close enough that if he breathed, she'd feel it. He didn't breathe. He glanced at her lips.

'I think I know what you mean.' She spoke softly, her eyes on his lips. 'But you're going to have to tell me.'

He cleared his throat, eyes suddenly aware of others in the restaurant. 'Are you coming out to the station this weekend?'

She straightened and grinned. 'If I get this case wrapped up.'

'Let's hope you do then.'

Chapter 44

The motel coffee provided a caffeine fix, but Jenny still needed her regular caramel latte before continuing her hunt.

Standing in the café, she tapped out a text message to Penny.

'One caramel latte.' Niko grinned as the patron waiting to order cringed at the announcement of Jenny's signature coffee.

'Thanks Niko. You have no idea how much I need this.'

'As much as you always do, no doubt.'

Jenny paid while taking a savouring sip. 'See ya.' Placing her card back into the top pocket of her utility vest, she checked her phone was secure and left the café.

A text came back before she could take another sip of her coffee. Checking her phone, she raised an eyebrow. Penny wasn't a morning person, but her friend obviously pulled out all stops to get her what she needed.

Blood type matched. DNA will be a while. Hope it helps!

Jenny typed back two emoji kissy faces before checking her notes to find the number she needed.

'Hello.' The voice was familiar. Just the person she was hoping to reach.

'Mr Newman. I'm sorry to disturb you at home. It's Constable Williams, from Coober Pedy.'

'Yes. What do you want Constable?'

She hadn't thought about how she was going to broach this subject. She couldn't exactly announce that Michael Newman was likely dead. What if he wasn't? What if her theory was totally wrong?

'Sir, have you heard from your son this week?'

'No. I've not heard from him for over a week.'

'Mr Newman, you didn't give us the information we needed, but you probably know by now that Michael is part of our investigation, but I'm worried Sir. For various reasons. We've been able to access his phone and credit-card records.'

'They better be damn good reasons Constable.'

Spoken like a true lawyer.

'They are Sir. I assure you, you would know. Judges don't issue warrants for no reason. Anyway. My point is, Michael hasn't used his credit-cards or phone all week, not since last Saturday. We have a BOLO out on his car, but I'd like your permission to search it if we find it Sir. It is your property.'

'Nothing since Saturday you say?' The man's voiced quivered. He was worried. That was her intention, but she didn't relish it. But a worried parent would be more inclined to cooperate.

'No Sir.'

'I'll do you one better.' She could hear tapping on a keyboard. 'The Audi has GPS tracking on board.' More keys tapped. 'I'll give this to you on one condition Constable.'

Jenny wasn't sure what he was going to give her, but she waited to hear what he wanted. When he said nothing, she prompted.

'What condition?'

'When you find him, you don't question him until I get there. You understand?'

'Of course Sir.' Jenny's gut knotted. Her instincts told her they weren't going to find Michael Newman, at least not alive. But she needed to know where the Audi was so she kept that revelation to herself.

'I have the GPS coordinates for the Audi, I'll text them to this mobile number.' He tapped keys again. Jenny's phone pinged in her ear.

'Remember Constable. Not one question without myself or one of my legal team present.'

She couldn't help but take the opportunity to test the water. 'Does that include Samantha Hayes Sir?'

'No. It most certainly does not include Hayes.'

'Of course Sir. I'll be in touch if we find him.'

'You do that.' The line went dead. Jenny pulled up the text message, gulped down the last of her coffee and jumped excitedly as the caffeine and adrenalin hit her system together.

She called the station and waited.

'Coober Pedy Police Station. Senior Constable O'Connell speaking.'

'Sir. I've got the GPS coordinates of the Audi. Do you want me to call Philips?'

'How on earth… Don't answer that. I'll call him. You send the coordinates and I'll get him to meet you there. Be careful Williams. Hayes and or Roberts could be with that vehicle.'

'I'm counting on it Sir.'

Chapter 45

Tapping her map, Jenny added the coordinates and waited the extraordinarily long time for the map to refresh before zooming in to read the location.

Coober Pedy wasn't large. There were the two main motels in town, a few caravan and camping parks, and a myriad of BnB options from retreats to quaint underground accommodation spots.

The coordinates where the Audi last pinged a satellite guided her out of town. A dust cloud followed her as she pulled off the main Sturt Highway and drove into an area with a mix of mines, vacant allotments and privately run accommodation locations. Pulling up at the last known GPS reading, she found an underground yoga retreat and spa.

Jenny fought the urge to go straight in and search for the Audi. Instead, she parked up the road in her vintage Dodge truck and waited for Philips to arrive in O'Connell's police Landcruiser.

She was keen to get out to Nick's place, to track the vehicle that chased them down and to clear the scene so Nick could go home and sift through what was left of his house, but it would have to wait until the police forensic team arrived from Adelaide.

No doubt that's why Penny was on hand so early this morning. There was every likelihood she was on a plane right now, heading up to help process the Homestead and the William Creek Pub fire.

The wait was frustrating. Glancing up, she noticed Philips driving up behind. Hopping out, she locked her car as he pulled up alongside.

'I can't see the car?' He spoke as Jenny jumped into the passenger's side.

'They likely parked it out of sight, but,' she held the phone up for him to see, 'this is where it last pinged.'

'If Roberts is shacked up with Hayes, there'll be no guessing what they've been up to.'

'I don't think that's ever been in doubt. The woman is hot, and she knows it. First she gets Newman doing her bidding and now it seems she's managed to twist a Major Crimes detective around her tiny little pinkie.' Jenny wiggled her own to make the point.

Philips drove the Landcruiser down the dirt driveway, lined with Sturt Desert Pea and other wild flowers from the recent rain. The sight of the dark red and black buds was glorious. The car pulled to a stop outside a coloured steel shed. Potted palms lined the doorway under a bullnose veranda with chimes that swayed in the light morning breeze.

Jenny could hear the tinkle, tinkle of crystals as they approached the front door. A sign reading *Ring for Service* sat wedged in the window. The restored wooden door featured frosted glass at the top half with the name of the retreat.

A brushed brass bell hung to the right of the door. Philips pulled the small rope back and forth while Jenny scoped out the side of the building. The drought-proof gardens were cared for. The shed wasn't large and there were no outbuildings. No doubt the entire retreat was below ground.

'I'm coming! I'm coming!' A woman's voice sounded annoyed from beyond the door.

'Not so Zen like.' Philips chuckled as Jenny stepped alongside him. They stood back from the door to give themselves and the occupant space.

'We're not open….' The door flew open. 'Oh.' The woman was dressed in short yoga pants and a sports top, her hair up in curlers. 'Officers. What can I do for you?'

'Sorry to bother you so early.' Philips didn't use the owner's name which led Jenny to believe she must have been new to the area. Maybe the business was also new? 'I'm Constable Philips, this is Constable Williams. We'd like to know if you have guests staying at the moment?'

The woman looked Jenny up and down before answering. 'Yes, a lovely couple.'

'Can you tell me where they are staying? Where their car might be parked?' Philips continued.

'I don't know. Am I supposed to give that sort of information out?'

'Well it's not confidential, if that's what you mean?' Jenny interceded, hoping to prevent the woman asking for due cause or a warrant. 'All accommodation operators are required to record the name and vehicle registration number of their guests. We are following up on a vehicle that's gone missing.'

The woman sucked in a breath. 'You mean stolen?' Her hand flew to her mouth. Philips realised what Jenny was up to. Thankfully he said nothing. They let the woman jump to her own conclusions. 'Oh my. The only vehicle here is a black Audi. Pretty car. I can't imagine the couple staying would have stolen it?'

'Where is the vehicle? And where are the occupants?'

The woman peered out the front door, from left to right as though she were hoping the neighbours couldn't see what was happening.

'They must be out.'

'So the car isn't here?'

'The Audi?'

'Yes. The Audi.'

'No that's here?' Jenny shook her head slightly, trying to understand what the woman was

saying.

'How do you know they are out then?'

'Because they had a four-wheel drive with them too. The man drove it in, the woman drove the Audi.'

Jenny's mind was doing summersaults. The car that tried to run them off the road. Surely, they couldn't be this lucky. 'Did you get the registration number for the four-wheel drive *and* the Audi?'

'Yes, of course.'

'Can we have it, along with access to the accommodation please.' The woman was rooted to the spot, her mouth hanging open.

'And can you show us where the Audi is?'

Chapter 46

The contents of the accommodation were boxed up for evidence. Two suitcases, a few pieces of loose clothing, bed linen and the toiletries from the bathroom.

O'Connell was running the registration number of the four-wheel drive. It was her hope they could link it to Roberts. Maybe then they would be able to get the warrant they needed to search Roberts' financials and phone records.

Jenny's phone pinged in her pocket. She checked the text as a tow-truck pulled into the driveway. Pushing her phone back into her vest pocket, she jogged towards her partner.

'Philips. Can you organise this?' She nodded at the truck. 'O'Connell wants me to grab Penny from the airport.'

'You got it.' He waved, pencil in hand as he recorded the resort owner's statement.

'Keep the scene closed and taped. I'll bring Penny out here to go over the place as soon as I can.'

'All good.' She could hear the owner complaining as she trudged up the driveway to where she left her car.

Twenty minutes later she pulled up to the airport as Penny walked out of the small clad building Coober Pedy claimed was a terminal. Barely larger than a schoolhouse, it boasted a few chairs, a vending machine and two airline counters.

Jumping out the driver's side, she rushed to meet Penny at the passenger's side door.

'Sorry. I was tied up on scene.'

'You've been busy I hear.'

'Too busy. I've hardly slept in the past two days. But I think we are getting close.'

'That's good news. As much as I love visiting you, I'm not that in love with this weather. It's going to be another scorcher.'

'Oh, that sucks big time.' The last thing they needed with a pyromaniac on the loose was blazing hot weather. 'Sorry again!'

Penny chuckled as Jenny grabbed her two forensic kit bags and popped them in the truck tray.

'Can I take you straight out to a scene? We've got a car coming in for inspection, but the accommodation operator would like to get her unit back up for rent as soon as possible.'

'Sounds fine.'

'I wasn't sure how long you'd be so I've taken all the photos. Starting with the room as a whole, then I've narrowed in on anything interesting as I've bagged it.'

'Excellent. We'll make a forensic crime-scene investigator of you yet.'

'I hope I didn't mess anything up. With this guy being a detective, I need to tick every box.'

'You'll be sweet. I know how meticulous you are. What have you got on Roberts?'

Jenny snapped her seatbelt in place, turned the key and started talking all in one smooth action.

'Not enough yet. But if we are right, his prints will be all over this place, which on their own, isn't enough for a warrant to search his financials, but if he's been driving the Audi, then we should be able to get it. Plus, O'Connell is trying to confirm Roberts purchased a burner phone that appears on Hayes' and Newman's phone records and we have another vehicle registration we are running.'

'The Audi?' Penny frowned as she clipped her belt on.

'I'll catch you up on the way.'

Jenny drove her car down the sloping driveway this time, parking in front of the accommodation entrance as the tow-truck pulled away with the Audi on the back.

'How long will the truck DNA take?' The Dodge door creaked as she opened it to step out.

'I've put a rush on it, but still could be a week.'

'That's a rush?'

'The labs are snowed under.' Penny pulled her bags from the rear tray. 'They work on a case-by-case basis and anything due to go to court gets top priority.'

'It's all yours. I'm heading back now.' Philips waved as they switched shifts.

'We won't be long Philips. I'll dust for prints and be back to process the boxes of evidence and the car. Can I have my old room at the station back?'

'It's still full of your gear.' Philips grinned as he pressed the unlock on his key fob and jumped into the police four-wheel drive.

'Can you ask O'Connell if he's got the info on that four-wheel drive rego yet?' Jenny called before he could close the door.

'I'm sure he'll call you as soon as we know who it belongs to.'

'How long does it take to run a rego?' Jenny rolled her eyes at Penny.

'Could be a hire car. He might need to check with the hire company.' Penny was right. It didn't make the wait any easier. 'Okay. Let's get to it then.'

Jenny pulled on a pair of gloves, Penny did the same, adding shoe protectors that Jenny didn't have earlier. She worried over where she stepped, what she did. Her nerves were frayed as she wondered if she contaminated anything. If she nailed Roberts, he'd be sure to find any holes she left in her investigation.

'Walk me through it.' Penny asked as they travelled below ground, into the dugout. Wall lights illuminated the multi coloured stone walls. Rough-sawn timber beams decorated the roof, but Jenny knew they weren't necessary from a structural standpoint. They were likely added for décor.

'Okay. I've bagged the bed linen. There's only one bed, so I'm sure fluids will indicate the relationship went further than friends.'

'Two single, able bodied human beings. That's pretty likely.'

'There was nothing obviously out of order. Two toothbrushes, male and female hygiene products. All bagged.'

'Okay. Let me dust everything for prints and then we can get out of here.'

Chapter 47

The murder board faced away from the front counter in the centre of the station office area.

'We have this photo of Roberts hiring the four-wheel drive. Rental agency said it hasn't been returned yet.' O'Connell stuck the picture to the whiteboard as he briefed the team.

'We have his prints in the Audi, in the unit and Penny confirms bodily fluids were found on the bed linen. We'll need DNA for a court case, but for now, it's clear Roberts has been sleeping with Hayes.' Jenny wrote on the whiteboard, her eyes scanning faces as she spoke.

'That's not enough to nail him with murder.' Sergeant Mackenzie said as he leant on the corner of the main desk.

Philips leant against the front counter, watching for customers, listening to the summary from a distance.

Jenny hovered over the whiteboard, hoping it would yield more answers.

'We need to start putting pieces together.' She scanned Sarge's face. He nodded for her to continue. 'Hayes was in cahoots with Newman. Let's say they smuggle babies into the country, make a killing, all off the books from the law firm she works at. Rachel finds out what's going on, runs, then Curtis sees an easy pay packet and starts blackmailing them.

'Roberts warns Curtis to get lost. That's maybe his way of not having to kill them, but someone killed Melinda, because she saw Newman die, or because someone thought she was carrying the evidence.'

'All sounds plausible Williams, but we need to prove it and we have no physical evidence linking any of them to our victim's murder.' Sarge pushed to his feet, strutted over, crossed his arms and huffed at the murder board like it was the enemy.

'Well we need Roberts' financials Sir, then we need to interview him and Hayes. Do we have a warrant yet?'

'Not yet. We'll get it, but we need to find them first.' O'Connell peered over his spectacles.

'That hire car is the key Sir and the SIM card.' Jenny stepped toward her locker, knowing the meeting was done.'

'Head back out to the William Creek Station. See if you can find any tracks from there. Follow them. I'll call around the local cattle properties and see if anyone has seen the four-wheel drive hire vehicle around the place.'

'With a broken headlight and smashed front end,' Jenny added as she pulled her vest over her head and opened the gun safe.

'And that. Yes. Get going. Take Nick back out there with you and once you and Penny are done, give him the all-clear to clean up his place. I'll call the C.F.S. in when you're ready, so let me know.'

'Thanks Boss. Will do.' Jenny saluted and caught Penny's eye to move out.

****

Jenny could see Nick's truck still parked outside the police station. Her earlier conversation ran through her mind. When she requested the transfer to Coober Pedy, solving her family mystery was all she could think about, but now. Now things were different.

So far, neither of them were bold enough to see if their relationship was more than just bonding over their family history. Or is that what Nick was trying to say at breakfast? Now more than ever, she wished her cousin was around.

Melanie would have known what to do. Her memories of her vivacious cousin were of a petite, cute teenager with no qualms about sharing how she felt, but now she was a grown woman, she wondered if she missed something about Melanie and her family. Something that could be the link to why they holidayed in the middle of the desert instead of a sun-drenched beach somewhere.

'What are we doing?' Penny's voice pulled her out of her daydream.

'Finding Nick. Seeing if he needs a lift home.'

'Why? Is his car broken down?'

'Long story, but we came to town in that old truck last night.'

'I think I need a glass of wine while you tell that story.'

'I know you do.' Jenny popped her head into Reception. 'Marj.'

'Jenny.' Marj's head snapped up, her bright smile matched by her bright red lipstick. 'Penny too. Good to see you too. What can I do for you lovely ladies?'

'Has Nick checked out yet?'

'Nope. He's in room twelve.'

'My old room.'

'Yes. I thought it was fitting.' She grinned, Penny chuckled and Jenny sighed. It seemed everyone except her and Nick were good at matchmaking.

'Thanks Marj.' Jenny stepped back out, and carried on down the covered walkway to Nick's room. Stopping outside, she knocked tentatively.

'Coming.'

'I wonder how Hayes overpowered and killed Newman?' Jenny wondered aloud.

'You don't know he's dead.'

'You're the one who found his blood type.'

'But no DNA yet.' Penny shook her head.

The door opened to reveal Nick in the same clothes he'd worn last night, but his hair was damp. At least he found time for a shower.

'We are heading back to your place, to run some forensic tests, photograph the scene. That stuff. Can we give you a lift? I figured the truck could use a rest.' Penny held back, leaning against a post on the veranda, her eyes scanning the artificial lawn and native hedge.

'Yeah, it barely made the long trip last night. I've booked it in for a service. Thanks for the offer, but Sam's coming in to pick me up. He stayed at the pub last night with Mick.' There was a sadness in Nick's eyes.

'How is he coping with the news?' Jenny wanted to reach out and touch his hand.

Nick sighed softly. 'I'll know more when I see him. You two head out there. Sam won't be long. I was just checking out.'

'Okay. If you're sure.'

'I'm good. Ed and Al, along with a few other boys are due back from muster later. We'll start cleaning up and salvaging what we can. The old stone homestead might be reparable.'

'Sarge said to let him know. He'll get the C.F.S. crew out to help.'

'Thanks. That would be good.'

'We'll see you soon then.' Jenny was riveted to the ground, while Nick seemed in no hurry to close the door. Penny cleared her throat.

'We've got lots of work to do.'

'Yeah, sorry. And a long way to drive.' She waved awkwardly as she stepped back from the door. 'Bye.'

'You two really should get your act together.' Thankfully Penny spoke after Nick closed the door.

'What are you talking about?' As soon as the question left her lips, she realised she should have ignored the comment.

'Don't play coy.' Penny shoved her playfully. 'You know what I'm talking about.'

Jenny sighed. 'It's not that simple.'

'Yes, it is. Male and female, healthy, attracted to each other. Just get on with it.'

Jenny waved her hand dismissively. Now was not the time to be thinking about romance. Now was the time to catch a dirty cop who might have killed an innocent woman and scared the hell out of two other people.

Chapter 48

Two hours of listening to Penny talk about Adelaide only made Jenny homesick. She needed to call her dad and let him know she was getting closer to finding out what happened to her cousin.

They drove down the dirt track, making their way toward the station outbuildings. The burnt-out remains of the homestead stood resolute. Ringlets of smoke floated skyward. The stone walls were intact, while the timber rafters fell all around the building. Windows were broken, frames charred.

'Nick is going to be heartbroken.'

'We need to find the point of origin. What fuel was used?' Penny stepped out, leant over the Dodge tray and reached for her forensic kit. Pulling it out the back of Jenny's truck, she turned and strode away.

'I'll take photos if you want,' Jenny called after her.

'That would be good. Where did the fire start?'

Jenny spotted Philips' Landcruiser as she followed Penny. The vehicle was parked close to the Homestead. Debris and heat left it unusable. Nick's car was right behind, less affected, but still damaged, the tyres burst from the extreme heat.

As if losing his home wasn't enough, now Nick's car was almost written off.

She gazed back at the homestead to see Penny waiting patiently. 'Sorry. Out front, then an explosion out the back, near the kitchen sliding doors. Nick said something about haystacks being set alight.'

'Check for tracks too. If you find any, let me know. I'll take castings.'

'Okay.'

Penny squatted down to take samples from outside – what were once the beautiful wooden double front doors of the homestead. Mangled roofing hung burnt and charred where the veranda posts once stood. Jenny drew a deep breath, then began taking photos around the exterior, finishing up outside, with what was left of the kitchen extension.

A lump wedged in her throat as hot tears stung her eyes. The huge glass doors that framed the escarpment view out the back of Nick's home were shattered, charred and warped. Scorch marks licked the sandstone bricks, leaving angry tendrils all along the pale ochre walls.

She sucked in a quick breath, wiped the tears from her eyes and stepped from the small patch of green grass, singed at the edges by the heat, on to the red dirt. Tyre tracks were visible in the daylight, but Jenny didn't recall seeing a car parked up in this spot. It wasn't somewhere the farm hands would usually park.

'Hey Penny. I think I've got tracks.' She snapped a few photos while she waited for the forensic scientist to come around the house.

Penny peered over Jenny's shoulder. 'Yep. I'll take a casting.'

'I'll follow them.'

Goose bumps broke out on her skin as she crept toward a machinery shed, following the tracks. Stopping outside, she photographed the tracks running inside the shed before hanging the camera around her neck, ready to open the doors.

Her hand was on the sliding door handle when she heard a car approach out front. Sam's classic dark blue Nissan Patrol with wide wheels and raised suspension growled up toward the house.

She smiled. The car was the same model her dad drove when she was a kid. Now it was considered a collectable. Worth more than some new cars.

Distracted, she left the shed door to greet the Johnston brothers. Sam was close to tears as he stepped out of his car. Nick's stone-cold fixed expression was back. The same one she now understood he put on when he didn't want to show any emotion.

'This sucks!' Sam slammed the car door closed. 'Who the hell would burn down our place?'

'Someone trying to kill Jenny and her witnesses mate. Just be glad we all got out alive.'

'Yeah. Sorry.' Sam watched his feet as they made circles in the dry, red earth.

'It's okay Sam. I get it. I'll catch the bastard. I promise.' She resisted the urge to give him a hug. The nineteen-year-old sighed, his shoulders dropped, but he lifted his gaze to meet hers.

She noticed Penny following the tracks she abandoned a moment before. 'I'll check it out Penny. Sorry. Got side-tracked.' She rushed toward the shed, berating herself for not staying focussed.

'It's okay. I've got it.' Penny called back. The door rattled and echoed as she slid it open, pulling her flashlight out and turning it on as she disappeared inside.

Jenny was halfway back when she heard a loud crash, followed by a male voice, then a scream. 'Penny.' She sprinted for the door arriving as Penny's flashlight rolled out, over the door tracks and spun in a circle on the dirt.

Chapter 49

The boys caught up to her as she reached the shed.

'Stop!' She pulled up, turning toward them, her hand held up. Unclipping her gun, she put her hand on the hilt and stalked forward.

Nick disappeared from her peripheral vision on the left. Sam was on her right. Where was Nick going?'

'You are a pain in my arse Williams.' Roberts appeared, Penny held close to his chest, her mouth clamped shut by his hand, a gun at her ribs. 'Take your gun out slowly, by the hilt and put it on the ground.'

'You know I can't do that.'

He jabbed the gun into Penny's ribs. She winced. 'You know I'll do it.'

'Why? All we've got on you so far is sleeping with Hayes.'

Roberts smirked but it failed to reach his eyes. 'And I'm sure you've tracked down that I was the one who hired that four-wheel drive.' He indicated behind him with his head. 'You're good. I'll give you that.'

Jenny pulled her gun out as instructed. The last thing she wanted to do was surrender her weapon, but Roberts was a cop. He knew all the tricks – some Jenny was yet to learn.

'That's it, now kick it to me.'

Jenny did as she was asked, but made sure the gun was far enough away Roberts couldn't collect it up.

'Where's Hayes?'

'Samantha!' Roberts called out in answer.

'You idiot.' Samantha Hayes might be slim, but the weight of her voice was not feather light. She was pissed off with being caught out. 'Now we'll need to kill them all.'

'I don't think so.' Sam lunged forward with the wisdom of youth.

'Sam. No!' Jenny grabbed his arm. 'Don't. He's a cop. A filthy, dirty one, but he won't hesitate to use that gun.'

'I wouldn't say that.' Roberts grimaced at her comment. 'I've not murdered anyone.'

'Shut up!' Samantha slapped the back of his head. 'You stuffed up at every turn.'

'But I didn't kill anyone.' He was fishing, Jenny could sense it. He wanted Samantha to admit she was the one that killed Newman and Melinda.

'You might as well have. You're in this up to your neck. Get us out of here.'

'How do you propose I do that councillor?'

'Negotiate.' Hayes was flustered, her cheeks flushed, her eyes wild.

'That's your department.' While Roberts was calm, methodical. Jenny could see he was planning something. The way his eyes kept peering over her shoulder, taking in his surroundings.

Samantha was out of place in her silk shirt, wedged heels and pencil thin skirt. Her hair was scruffy, no doubt from sleeping in the car for the night, but otherwise, she looked like she stepped out on her way to the office in the morning.

'I paid you a fortune. Get us a plane or something!'

'You honestly think it's that easy? Flight plans need to be lodged. This isn't some stupid movie where we fly out to the Caribbean. You blackmailed me into playing along with your plans, but I didn't sign on for murder. I didn't kill Newman or Melinda.'

He was trying to get her to admit to killing them. He wanted an out. At least from murder.

'Look. We know about the adoption scam.' Jenny's gaze fixed on the lawyer, who ripped her eyes away from Roberts, her face contorted in a snarl.

'You've got squat.' The posh accent was gone.

'We have a micro-USB with all the documents Rachel took from your office. We have your travel records. We also know you never boarded the plane from Melbourne to Coober Pedy, so you were here, in town, when Melinda was killed.

'Roberts' intervention is the only reason we've not arrested you already. Your Harlequin connection has given you anonymity up until this point. But my boss is already in discussions with the Federal police. The A.F.P. might cut you a deal for what you know, but you are going to jail Ms Hayes. It's up to you how many counts of murder you add to the charges. Too many and the A.F.P. won't be able to deal with you. Without protective custody, the Harlequins will see you dead in jail.'

'I'm giving you nothing little girl. You're way out of your league.' The lawyer's hands waved wildly.

Penny squirmed, but Roberts pushed the gun into her ribs. She pulled her hand out of her pocket. Jenny watched her eyes dart down to the pocket, then back up again, her eyes intense.

What was she trying to tell her?

'This has gone far enough. Killing two cops, and a nineteen-year-old kid is only going to make the hunt for you deadly, and ruin any chance of brokering a deal with the Feds.'

'She's right.' Roberts offered casually, but the gun was still against Penny's ribs.

Jenny eyed her pistol on the ground, too far away from her to reach quickly. Penny's gun was gone, likely inside the shed somewhere.

Where was Nick?

'I didn't have a choice you know. The money was good, and the sex was okay, but my hands were tied.'

Samantha punched his arm, hard. The cop didn't even wince. 'Okay! You've never had it so good.'

She was seething. Was it the comment or his betrayal? So far, Hayes hadn't disputed anything Roberts said and she seemed happy enough to end all their lives.

Cold Bitch!

'If you didn't kill anyone, why don't you give me the gun and we can sort it out,' Jenny offered.

'Don't you dare!' Hayes stepped toward Jenny's weapon, leant down and grabbed it, aiming it at Roberts.

'Don't!' Jenny begged. Penny was right in the line of fire. 'Stay calm. I can organise a plane. William Creek Pub gets small aircraft flying in all the time.'

Roberts laughed aloud. 'Since when do cops negotiate with killers?'

'Since they started holding my friend hostage.' Jenny spat the words.

'I told you. I'm not a killer.' Roberts' tone was still calm. Like he was executing a well-made plan. *Maybe he was?*

'That's what you said about Hayes. If you're not a killer, then let Penny go.'

'I can't do that. Even if I plead out, I'll be stuck in prison and I'm a cop. I've put a lot of guys in that hole.'

'You should have thought about it before taking her money.' Jenny pointed to Hayes, still waving the gun in the air, annoyed that no one was taking her seriously. Jenny wondered if the woman was up to killing, the way she seemed hesitant to use the gun now.

Was Roberts acting again?

'You can turn over the Harlequins, Hayes's connections and I'm sure there's more dirt you have on someone you can offer. Campbell or Smart maybe? Hayes must have introduced you to enough leeches in her corporate world.'

Roberts smiled. 'Nice try.'

'What do you want then?'

'I want the keys to your car. Your stunt last night smashed the radiator on ours.'

'Who set fire to the homestead?' Sam lurched forward.

'Sam. Shut up. Please!' she begged, her hand on his arm. He huffed, but slunk back.

'I knew you'd get out. You're a smart girl Williams.'

'You couldn't have guaranteed that.' She nearly said they wouldn't have gotten out if not for Nick, but maybe Roberts didn't know Nick was there. *Where was he anyway?*

A sound made Roberts turn. 'What's that?' His head flipped from side to side.

Sam started to speak, but Jenny spoke over him. 'I don't know.' She turned, glaring at Sam over her shoulder, warning him with her eyes to stay quiet.

'It's coming from over there.' Roberts waved the gun in the air. 'Go find out,' he directed Hayes.

'I'm not going anywhere. You're trying to sell me out. You think I was born yesterday? I'm a criminal attorney you twit.'

The sound grew louder and Jenny knew exactly what it was. Dust rose around them as Nick's chopper came into view, flying low across the ground. Visibility was lost in a heartbeat.

'Stay out the way Sam.' Jenny hoped the hot-blooded teen wouldn't let delusions of heroism get out of control. The last thing she wanted was for Nick to lose his brother along with everyone and everything else.

Jenny heard Roberts grunt. She could barely see the outline of Hayes amongst the spiralling red dust. The woman was armed, but was she willing to use the gun? Jenny had to take the risk. A gun shot sounded, she ducked instinctively.

'Get down Sam,' she screamed over the sound of the chopper circling overhead, stirring up as much dust as possible. Her heart pounded, sweat broke out, her ears rang but all other sound left her as she stalked Hayes.

Keeping low to avoid the waving gun, she dived at the lawyer's legs, taking them out from under her with her sheer weight and speed.

'Stay down.' She grabbed the gun hand and thumped it on the ground until the lawyer let go. Wrenching her arm around behind her back, she didn't hold back.

Hayes screamed. 'Let go you bitch. Let me go!' Jenny could hear Roberts and Penny tussling next to her but visibility was impossible. The sound of a slap, followed by a thud told her someone was down.

A soft moan sounded a few metres away. Penny was hurt. She dragged Hayes's other arm around hard, pulled her cuffs from her vest and snapped them shut tightly around one wrist. Standing, she dragged Hayes up by her arms, onto her knees.

'Stand up. Now!' Jenny yelled. Hayes growled like a dog, but did as she was told. 'Over here.' She dragged her through the dust as it filled her nose and ears. Shielding her eyes with her spare hand, she peered into the dust. Visibility was next to zero, but in her mind's eye, she could see the metal handle on the shed door.

She ran her hand in circles, her palm flat on the metal until it hit the handle. She shoved Hayes face-first into the wall, threaded the cuffs through the handle and clamped them shut on the lawyer's other wrist.

The dust continued to rise, but Nick must have seen something. The chopper drifted away from the shed, toward the homestead.

Roberts must be running!

Jenny spun around, searching for Penny and Sam.

The dust started to settle. 'Make sure she doesn't go anywhere and check on Penny.' She called to Sam as she sprinted toward the homestead.

About ten metres from the ruins she realised she forgot to grab her gun. Did Roberts still have his? God, she hoped not.

'You'll be hunted for the rest of your life Roberts,' she called into the dust cloud Nick now created over her Dodge.

'Better than being shanked in jail.' She followed his voice in the dust cloud.

'You can turn over the evidence we need on Hayes. Without it, she'll likely walk on the murders. All we've got is the illegal adoption records.'

She waved for Nick to get away, hoping he could see her in the spiralling haze of red dirt. 'You don't have the keys.' She yelled, then choked on the dust. Tears sprang to her eyes, reminiscent of the fires she endured. Fire set by Roberts to look like Newman was alive.

'I'll get to you before you can hotwire it.' Time stood still as Roberts stayed silent and the chopper hovered overhead. Then it flew away.

'You know it's your best bet. Give us what we need. I'm sure you have something else to bargain. Is Campbell clean? Smart never took our calls. Maybe you know something about that?'

The dust settled to reveal Roberts standing by her car, the door still closed.

'I said you were good.' His lip was curved in a weak smile, but his eyes were sad, regretful.

'We've got her recorded.' Penny approached, a mobile phone in her hand, a smile across her already bruising face.

'You don't need me then.' He opened the door.

'She didn't confess to the murders Roberts. Only her intent to kill us. We need your testimony. You've got nowhere to go. The Harlequins will want you dead when they find out you were undercover. The cops won't stop hunting. We need your testimony. You can answer the unanswerable questions. Who killed Melinda? Was it Newman or Hayes? You'll be on the run forever. Make a deal with me Roberts.'

'You're not going anywhere detective.' Penny held a gun in both hands. Sam handed Jenny her service weapon.

Roberts' chest rose with a deep, thoughtful breath, his hand still on the door handle. 'I could make you shoot me.'

'Why would you do that?' Jenny put her gun back in her holster. Placing her hand on top of Penny's weapon, she indicated for the scientist to do the same, wondering in the back of her mind when was the last time Penny submitted to weapons testing or training.

'You're not a murderer Roberts. I can feel it in my bones.'

'You're too young for that.'

'Maybe. Do we have a deal?' She studied him closely. Every muscle in his body was taught, ready to act.

Roberts watched her suspiciously. Then visibly relaxed, removing his hand from the door handle. 'I got in too deep with Hayes, but I desperately wanted to bring the Harlequins down.'

'I could see that.' She threw him a thick, police issue cable tie. 'Use your teeth on it if you have to.' She wasn't going anywhere near him.

The detective fed the cable tie end in, placed his hands inside and pulled it tight with his teeth. 'You'll make a great detective one day Williams.'

'You'll excuse me if I don't put too much value in your opinion Roberts.'

Chapter 50

Jenny sat on the bonnet of Philips' burnt out Cruiser, a drink of cool water from a plastic cup soothing her parched throat. Her eyes were fixed on Nick as he gave his statement to two detectives from Adelaide.

The larger detective squinted at her. His expression wavered between suspicion and admiration. The other recorded her statement earlier. His piercing blue eyes studied her intently throughout the interview.

Both were sharp. Both gave her cause to consider training to be a detective, if she ever solved her cousin's case.

'You look knackered.' Penny wrapped an arm around her shoulder and squeezed.

'You don't look much better.' They laughed.

'Is the recording enough?'

'With Roberts' statement, I think it will put Hayes behind bars for a very long time.'

'Who killed Newman?'

'Hayes killed Newman in a fit of rage after he set Melinda alight in a public place. I don't think Roberts saw any of this coming. He's confirmed Newman was in the truck fire. I think he lit it up. I can't see Hayes getting her hands dirty.'

'I think you're right there.' They glanced at the woman with the silk shirt, now covered in red dust, standing by the detective's vehicle.' What I don't get is why Roberts got himself mixed up with an illegal adoption ring.'

Jenny sighed, sadness touched her heart, making it difficult to breathe. Her limbs were heavy and slow to react. Or was it the lack of sleep or abating adrenalin?

'Roberts wanted the Harlequins so bad. He thought he was using Hayes, but she used him. She's got a lot of clout with the gang – threatened to expose him.'

Penny's mouth gaped open. 'She blackmailed him. What! Cover up her mess, and guarantee her immunity from prosecution? Will that hold up now?'

'I don't think so, but that's not up to us. Melinda's murderer is dead. His murderer will be charged. Roberts will do a deal. No one wants to put a cop behind bars if they can avoid it. He'll be useful to the A.F.P..'

'Has anyone told Newman Senior, their junior partner is under arrest for killing Michael?'

'No. I'll leave that to the Adelaide detectives. Do you know them?'

'Sure. Jack Cunningham on the right. He's a top detective, straight down the line. His partner is Max Fitzpatrick. We call him grumpy, like the grumpy dwarf.' Penny laughed. 'By the way, I've lodged a request to reopen Nick's dad's case.'

Jenny's eyes locked on to Penny's 'That great. How? Why?'

'You remember the photo you showed me the other night, at the motel bar?' Jenny nodded. 'I didn't have time to study it properly, but something was wrong Jenny. I pulled the file when I got back to Adelaide. He shouldn't have fallen on the table if he shot himself. The wound on the back of his head in the picture appeared to be an entry, not exit wound. I'll know more once we exhume the body.'

'That's awesome.' Jenny saw Nick finishing up with his interview. His eyes sought her out, the frown of his brow deepened, his gaze locked on to her as he approached.

'Let me tell him?' Penny nodded. Jenny smiled at Nick. 'That was smart thinking, with the chopper.' He remained quiet, drawing closer, then stepping up into her personal space.

Penny cleared her throat, then hopped off the bonnet. 'Guess it's time to give my statement.' She skipped away. Jenny watched her and grinned.

'I wondered where you went for a minute.' His eyes drilled into her, seeking out the depths of her soul. Her breathing quickened. In her few months with Nick, she knew there was a connection, but this was different. This made her toes curl and her stomach do summersaults.

'I knew you wouldn't leave Sam in the lurch.' She kept babbling. He put his hands on her thighs, hesitated a moment, then wrapped his arms around her torso and drew her to him.

His voice was husky, on the edge of emotions he never usually showed. 'I'd never leave you exposed like that. You scared the hell out of me. Standing up to Roberts like that.' His mouth was so close, the warmth of his lips radiated, his words soft. Her skin tingled.

She licked her lips. Was he going to kiss her? Oh God she hoped so. 'It's my job.' She whispered back. 'Can you live with that?'

'Let's find out.' His lips brushed hers, feather light. She could smell his sweat, his faded aftershave – spicy. He brushed a loose piece of hair over her ear. The touch sent shivers down her spine.

Pulling back a little, his eyes studied her face. What was he waiting for? *Her of course*. He was waiting for her to respond. She lifted her chin. His lips touched hers again. She was over waiting.

Reaching up, she ran her hands up the back of his neck and pulled him into a full, deep, passionate kiss. He moaned, she couldn't think straight. She should have been embarrassed. She should have been searching the area for anyone watching, but she didn't care who saw them.

Nick drew back. 'This is going to be complicated.'

'Two hours apart is a long way.'

'Nothing for a chopper.' He smiled, that rare curve of his lips was becoming more common. She was very pleased to be on the receiving end. Leaning forward again, he kissed her deeply. Sighing, he pulled back, his forehead rested on hers.

'I have to go.' She spoke the words he knew were coming.

'I know.'

'I'll be back soon.'

'I know.'

****

Thanks for reading! I hope you enjoyed *Her Scorched Bones*. I'd love to see your review on your favourite online bookstore.

Her Hidden Bones - Book 4 in the *Opal Field* series is available from all good bookstores. If you would like to learn more about my writing or what's next in Jenny's story, then visit my website www.atime2write.com.au.

Printed in Great Britain
by Amazon

41586344R00131